KING OF NOTHING

A DARK RH ROMANCE PETER PAN RETELLING

BRUTAL NEVER BOYS 1

MONA BLACK

KING OF NOTHING
BRUTAL NEVER BOYS 1

No man has ever managed to satisfy me—until Peter Pan carries me away to Neverland and now all bets are off...

I never thought that there is another reality beyond this one. My life is normal—work, routine, a few disappointing flings—when a man grabs me from the street and carries me off to Neverland.

A madman.

Granted, he probably saved my life, and the island he has brought me to is beautiful, the sights including three more hunks like him.

He says his name is Peter Pan and this is Neverland, he says they have been waiting for me and I may be the one...

Yeah, he sounds like a madman, all right.

A pity. He's so *pretty*. And so are his friends.

Peter and the Lost Boys, living on an island where the mermaids sing in the sea and creatures named Reds roam the land.

It sounds like a fairytale.

But if Peter is mad, the rest aren't much better. Dark forces seem to be at work here, and I'm caught in a web of fear and doubt.

The Lost Boys turn out to be violent, vicious men and I am their plaything.

Caught in a web of desire and pleasure.

Am I really the one they have been expecting?

Can I save them?

And do I even want to?

NOTE: this book is first in a trilogy ending in a cliffy. It features mature situations with some dark themes and adult language. Warning for dubcon, blood, gun, & knife play, self-harm, violence, kidnapping, stalking, forced proximity, bondage, light BDSM, unhinged psycho men and M/M relationships. Also child abuse (past, off page) and rape involving the mains (past, off page). Only for +18 audiences.

The trilogy has been written and all three books will be released by June.

No AI was used in the creation of this book.

King of Nothing (Brutal Never Boys 1)

Copyright © Mona Black 2023

Published by Black Wing Press

"Would you like an adventure now or would like to have your tea first?"
Peter Pan (— J.M. Barrie)

PART I

"All the world is made of faith, and trust, and pixie dust."
— J.M. Barrie, Peter Pan

1

WENDY

The sound of crashing waves always comes first. Booming, roaring around me, deafening. As if I'm caught in the middle of a gale.

Then I feel the impact, the sudden forceful plunge into the cold, the water sucking me down, drowning me. Pressing on me.

Above me, as I claw at the glittering surface, trying to swim back up, I see a pair of filmy white eyes. Clawed hands reach for me, pale designs writhing on them. A fanged mouth opens.

Shadows slither around me, whispering, asking, murmuring. Monsters in the deep, grotesque faces, hungry, ravenous for flesh, for more, ready to suck out my soul...

Until a strong hand closes around my arm, hauling me up, up, out of the water and onto dry land, where I gasp and flail like a stranded fish. Someone is calling my name. Shaking me.

"Wendy..."

I want to run, scream in terror, my heart slamming about inside my chest—but a body slams me down to the ground, grinding on top of me.

There's a growl in my ear. *"Wendy, stop..."*

With a cry, I jerk awake from my usual nightmare and sit up in my narrow bed, drenched in sweat.

Not real, I tell myself, needing the reminder as the sky outside my small window turns gray.

Just a bad dream. This is real.

This dingy room, the humidity in the walls, your worn slippers and robe, your shift starting way too early and yet late for someone who can't sleep.

Except to dream of hell.

Rolling out of bed, I pad barefoot to the window, study the street below.

No shadows. Nobody watching me. Except for a tall, broad-shouldered figure huddled inside a store entrance, but I think... I think he's always been there. A homeless person. A junkie.

I must have dropped a coin into his palm once in a while.

I *think*.

Shaking my head, I turn away, a headache blooming behind my eyes. I rub at my brow as I shuffle past my roomie's door and into our tiny kitchenette. Gray light spills through the windows as I open cupboards hunting after my favorite drug.

The elixir of the gods.

You guessed it. Coffee. But oh, *shit*, we're almost out of the precious brown powder, I realize when I open the box where we keep it.

Oh no... But wait, there are a few spoonfuls left, so the world won't end today, after all.

Making a mental note to get another package after work, and maybe some ginger cookies, too, because Charlie likes them, I shovel coffee into the machine, pour in the water and start it brewing.

The gurgling sound it makes is soothing, though I really just hope it's not the sound of our coffee machine dying. My money is counted down to the last cent. Between rent, food and sending a monthly sum back home for my brothers, there's practically nothing left.

Broke as a joke.

Stop fretting over the money, I tell myself, taking out my favorite, chipped mug with the bunny ears from the shelf by the window. *The coffee machine won't break down. You won't lose your job. Charlie won't jump ship. Don't imagine problems where there are none.*

Don't let your nightmares convince you that the world is ending.

Drinking my bitter brew, I knock on Charlie's—Charlotte's —door and get a sleepy greeting from inside.

It sounds like 'good morning,' but I hesitate. Her greeting doesn't fool me—the girl can talk in her sleep, and sometimes quite coherently, too. Her brain has apparently evolved to take care of things while she dreams away.

What I sometimes do is go inside and pull her covers off, but I actually hear steps inside her room which means she *is* awake today.

Strange! But that's good news. I don't have time to go through Charlie's summoning ritual today. I'm going to be late, despite waking up at the crack of dawn, and I need to get going.

So I hop into the shower and curse my life. The showerhead spits out cold and hot water in turns, making me jump and shudder. That's one way of clearing your head, I guess. And this isn't unusual behavior for our shower. It's old and has a personality.

A crappy personality. The shower is probably a guy.

"You and me, dear shower, are done," I tell it as I wash off the last of the soap and hop out. "It would never have worked between us."

Nor has it ever worked between me and any guy, but that's another story.

I never linger around naked anyway. The heater keeps acting up, and we're in the heart of winter. It's frigging cold.

Come on, I tell myself. *It could be worse.*

I could be in the sea, drowning.

I could still be living at home with my parents, but I got away.

That's a win, Dee, I tell myself.

And soon I'll get my brothers out, too. John will be sixteen soon. Leonard will be eighteen. They will be independent. No need for me to worry about them anymore.

The only good thing that comes out of being an adult is being able to run away and get yourself into your own messes. *Ha*. I'm actually doing okay, thank you.

But the moment I ran away was, of course, when my nightmares got worse.

Figures.

"Dee." Charlie comes out of her room as I pull on my boots and jacket, ruffling her curls. She yawns. "You're up early."

"Early? I'm *so* late," I mutter as I pull on my newest short skirt and my favorite sweater, then my thick socks and black low boots. "Late for work. Late for life."

She wanders into the kitchen, pours herself a cup of coffee, pads back out to rejoin me. "Are you?"

"Can't you see the time?" *Time.* I stop, frowning. A faint *tik-tock* rings in my ears, as if from a distant clock. "Hey, do you hear that?"

"Hear what? Listen, that guy hanging out outside..." Charlie yawns again. "God, I'm so sleepy. Is that your boyfriend or something?"

"Guy?" I turn my frown on her as I zip up my jacket and grab my handbag. "What guy?"

"I dunno. Just a guy. He's staring up at our apartment." She waves a negligent hand at the window and takes a sip from her coffee. "What happened to that yummy man you were going out with? James? Jimmy?"

"Jem? I never went out with him, Charlie."

"Oh. I could have sworn."

"We went on one date. Which went nowhere. I'm into travel shows and fantasy books. You know, a classic escapist. He's into himself."

She laughs, then winces. "Ow, that sounds familiar. Talked too much about himself, did he?"

"He did."

"Boring?"

"Like you wouldn't believe. Who cares about chassis and insulated returns, anyway? I wouldn't know one if it bit me in the ass."

"Ouch."

And it wasn't even that what put me off. The truth is that I did follow him to his expensive apartment and we did fall into bed. We kissed, we undressed, we touched, performed all the right moves, but there was no spark. Not on my side anyway.

It was... *dull*. Mechanical.

Oh, I made a pun!

Anyway, yeah, his life runs apparently like clockwork, his parents have money, his grades at college were good, his work prospects great. His looks are perfect, hair styled without a hair out of place, no acne pockmarks on his face, and his eyes...

His eyes are clear of shadows.

His moves were predictable, *careful*, as he unzipped my dress, took off my shoes and placed them by the bed, asked if he could kiss me.

Too careful.

Too gentle.

And what does that say about me, that I'm bored with a nice guy like him but wake up screaming from dreams of shadows?

"To be honest," Charlie says, gazing at me over the rim of her mug, "what I had meant was, finding faults with any guy you go out with feels familiar. You know?"

"Wow, gee, thanks, friend. I needed this today." I roll my eyes.

"Dee?"

"Hm. What?"

"Pull up your hood. It looks like snow." She shudders. "Ugh, cold. Gonna turn up the heating."

"No," I say automatically, "don't. It eats up too much electricity and—"

"—we don't have money," Charlie finishes with a sigh. "I know, babe, but turning into icicles won't help us make money, will it? Now go, shoo. Hey!" she calls as I open the door. "I hope you left me some hot water for the shower."

"Heater's acting up again," I mutter.

"Oh, no. Dammit." She pats her hair, checks her nails. "And I need to redo my nail polish. Got to keep up the appearances."

That's Charlie for you. She likes to go around looking cute and sexy, and she totally is, but sometimes I think it's all a façade, and that she's... not happy.

I wish I could help somehow, find out what she needs and help her get it, but if I can't fix myself, how am I ever going to fix her?

But I really am late by now, so frigging late, so I leave her standing there and rush down the stairs, skidding on the steps.

Charlie works in a beauty parlor so she has time before she has to get ready for work. Me, I work in a coffee shop and we open early to accommodate workers and office people.

If I'm late one more time, the boss is likely to fire me. Maybe that's what the nightmares are all about. Losing my job. Maybe the fangs and claws are poverty reaching for me like a blood-sucking vampire.

Stepping out onto the street is like being clawed, for sure, the cold digging its talons into my face.

Gah.

Huddling in my jacket, I glance up. The low-hanging clouds

look like snow. I can smell it on the air. Need to fix that heater or we'll freeze.

I bow my head against the whistling wind as I trudge down the street. The junkie isn't there anymore, I notice as I pass by the store—a closed-down, barred tobacco store. Not even a blanket or empty syringe marks the place where he was sitting earlier.

Or did I imagine it?

Shaking my head, I open my stride, remembering that I'm late and shouldn't worry about other people, not with my plate full like that. I need to keep my job until I find something better and until I can get my brothers out of the house, move somewhere as far away from the water as possible—away from lakes, ponds and the ocean—and then—

A man comes at me, wearing a black mask, pale hair and pale eyes visible underneath, raising his hand to grab me.

But he never reaches me. Something crashes into me, throwing me back.

A person, I think as I go flying backward, *another man*—and then a hand grabs my arm before I hit the ground, yanking me back up on my feet.

I sway as the man looms over me—I get a glimpse of short dark hair and piercing blue eyes, eyes like those haunting my nightmares—and then he lifts a blade in a tattooed hand and stabs me in the heart.

Oh, I think, *of course he goes for the heart.*

And this time I fall, and fall, and fall. *He stabbed me. Killed me.*

I'm dying.

I'm dead.

As blackness rushes in, his handsome face bends over me— thick dark brows, a hard jaw, lips pulled back to bare sharp teeth—and I try to scream but I'm gone.

2

WENDY

I open my eyes and the first thing I see is stars. Distant, blinking, silver stars on a dark sky, forming constellations, weaving the light into the fabric of night.

Wait, did I say *night*?

I blink, my chest tightening, my next breath cut short. Wasn't it morning just now? Wasn't I on my way to work? When did night fall?

Then I look down and realize that I'm not in my bed. Instead, I'm lying on sand.

A beach.

Shit. Shit! I sit up so quickly my head spins. Panic closes like a fist around my throat as I scramble to get away from the crashing waves, scooting up the beach.

I'm wet, my clothes clinging to my skin, and I've somehow lost my hood and jacket. My black stockings are filthy and get covered in sand as I scoot up the beach, as far away from the water as I can.

This is like one of my nightmares, and I hate how my heart is racing. It's pounding fit to break a rib. I don't want the water to touch me—and yeah, that always makes for a fun experience in the shower, whether the heater works right or not.

Like I said, I never linger under the water.

Not a water fan.

Finally, I get my feet under me and stand shakily up, only to notice a man lying prone on the beach a few feet away from me, hair and clothes wet. Black ink winds over the backs of his hands and up corded forearms.

I know his face.

He's the guy who attacked me, isn't he?

No, wait, this one must be the guy who intervened, right? Dark hair, right, this is the dark-haired guy who... who pulled me away, and then he...?

He stabbed me.

Jesus Christ.

Patting my chest, I stumble back a few steps.

But I'm alive. How can that be? Finally, I look down at myself. He stabbed me, didn't he? I remember it clearly, I remember how it felt—but there's no blood, no tear in my favorite blue sweater.

When I lift the hem, then my shirt, too, I find my skin smooth and unmarred underneath.

Did I imagine it?

Must have.

I grab my own pendant, cradling the silver thimble hanging from the chain in my hand, and I draw a shaky breath.

It doesn't matter. That bastard brought me here. Wherever this is. Even if I don't feel like I'm dying.

Though I do feel a little unsteady. How did we arrive here? And why is he out? Why are we both wet as if we swam to reach this beach?

"Hey!" I call out. "You. Guy."

He doesn't stir, and this time I take a step closer, my curiosity getting the better of me.

My first impression was that he's handsome, and closer inspection confirms it.

Yummy, as Charlie would have said, had she been here. *Very yummy.*

Tousled, dark hair, light stubble on his square jaw, long lashes resting on broad cheekbones. His mouth has an arrogant tilt, even passed out like he is. He has a thin golden chain around his neck with a small round pendant that looks like an acorn.

And those tats.

Yeah... He's pretty. Charlie wouldn't have just stared, like me. Oh, no, wait. She'd probably have already cuddled the passed-out stranger, wrapped her arms around his broad shoulders and asked him to take her to bed.

When his long, dark lashes flutter and those full lips part on an exhale, well, I admit I'm tempted, too.

No, Wendy. Jesus, what are you thinking?

That this is the most exciting thing that's happened to me since I left home?

Christ on a stick.

"Hey!" I call out again, looking around for a rock or something to use as a weapon. "Where's my handbag? What did you do with it? What...?"

I trail off, my breath catching in my throat as from the corner of my eye I see a creature crawling out of the water.

A mermaid.

Wait, what?

It's a monstrous thing, dragging itself up the beach with pale, skeletal arms, pulling a long fishtail behind it, trailing pale green hair, its face like a skull.

Black spots flash in my vision. What in the ever-loving *fuck*? What...? Is this real? Is it even possible? What's happening?

Dizzy, I stumble backward, then turn to the yummy guy, crouch down and grab his arm. It's thick with muscle and damn heavy. "Come on, wake up. Wake up! Get up, Jesus Christ, move!"

With a groan, he opens his eyes and gives me a bleary glare, then seems to focus on my face. "You," he breathes.

"No!" I yell at him, "not me. That... *thing* coming from the water. Is this a dream? Is this real? What the hell am I supposed to do?"

Because even in dreams you try to escape, even when you know you can't.

"Real? You're asking me if this place is real?" He gives a raucous laugh, then he coughs. "Holy shit."

"Yeah! Did you give me drugs, is this what this is? Am I seeing things? The beach, you, that... mermaid thing over there—"

"Mermaid. Did you just say *mermaid*?" His gaze sharpens instantly and he pushes himself off the sand with a grunt. "Fuck."

"Yeah, that's exactly what I said. *Fuck. Mermaid.* Not the prettiest of creatures. I..." I turn to look at the thing crawling up the beach at a good speed and shiver. "She's... real, isn't she? I'm not hallucinating, am I?"

"The mermaid is real," he growls, an honest-to-God growl —an echo from my latest nightmare—and then he's on his feet and hauling me up, too.

Whoa, he's tall, like, really tall, six feet four or something, solidly built and frigging gorgeous, though the white sand pressed to one side of his face is kind of funny.

Apart from the pale blue wolf-eyes, the square jaw and soft lips, he has ink all over him. Looks like he has full sleeves on his arms, ink on the back and sides of his neck, too, at least as much as I can see inside his unzipped black hoodie, as well as on the backs of his hands.

Hands that are currently grabbing me, breaking me out of

my stupor, and lifting me easily, slinging me over one of his shoulders like a bag of potatoes.

"Hey. Hey!" I beat at his muscular back with my fists as he starts moving. "What are you doing? Put me down!"

"Shut up," he snarls, slaps my ass and climbs up the beach toward tall dunes. "Or I drop you on the sand for the fucking mermaid to snack on."

I gape. He wouldn't! I hang on his shoulder like a limp noodle, and then think to turn my head sideways to take another look at the mermaid, and...

Yep. Still crawling toward us.

Holy crap.

God, that thing is ugly.

"Aren't mermaids supposed to be small and cute?" I mutter, give his back another hit with my fist. "Like Ariel. Curled up on rocks. Singing to the moon. This one is like a... a dead thing. Drowned and rotten. I'm Wendy by the way. Wendy—"

"Darling," he rumbles. "I know."

"You do?" I breathe.

"Oh, yeah."

"You know my name! What the hell, are you a creep? Who are you? Put me down!"

"I'm Peter," he says, not making any move to grant my wish, still marching up the beach, never breaking stride.

"Peter. Peter who? The Apostle? Peter Parker? Peter Jackson? Peter Rabbit? I don't know any Peters. Not in real life anyway. Charlie would know." I frown. "But wait, no, she wouldn't, because we don't know you. Get it?"

"You talk too much," he says, his voice flat.

"I *talk* too much? Jesus. Are you for real? Wait, don't answer that. I think... I think I'm in shock," I whisper. "Do you think I'm in shock?"

He says nothing and keeps going, between the dunes and out onto an overgrown path that runs through abandoned fields and scraggly trees, leading toward some ruins. His scent fills my senses, dark and musky with a hint of sea salt and engine oil.

I fist my hands in his soaked shirt and struggle to breathe around the scent, through it; through this stunning turn of events.

What is this place?

The ruins gleam in the light, pale and jagged. I only see them when the path twists and turns, and I catch glimpses of run-down buildings among trees, crumbling concrete walls covered in graffiti and abandoned cars.

Wait... why does it look familiar? Have I been here before? Or...

"I've dreamed of this," I whisper as the realization hits me. "Of dark water and horrible creatures living in it, chasing me. Of a town like this." I swallow hard as more things surface in my mind. "I dreamed of your eyes. How is that possible? I'm losing it, that's it, I'm losing it—"

"That's because this *is* your dream," he says, or at least that's what I think he says.

"What are you talking about? Who did you say you are? Peter? Peter who? What do you want with me? Where are we?"

No reply.

He's quiet for a long while, keeping a good pace toward the ruined city, his hold on my legs like steel—he remains quiet for so long, in fact, that I'm starting to think he won't ever speak to me again, just kill me and dump me in some ditch.

Maybe I talked too much and annoyed him. Who knows with psycho kidnappers, right?

Oh God, I really am going to die.

I start to hyperventilate, my grip on his wet shirt so tight my knuckles ache.

At some point, I realize that we have turned away from the ruins and are walking among trees. I can't take this suspense anymore. If he's going to end me, he'd better do it soon, or else my heart might give out.

I think I make a noise of despair, a suffocating noise, and he slows down. He doesn't ask if I'm okay, if I'm freaking out or having a heart attack.

Instead, he says, "I'm Peter Pan. But in this place, they call me *King*."

"This place?" I manage, still hanging upside down, still panicking. "What place is this?"

He gives a dark chuckle. "Welcome to Neverland."

3

PETER

S he squirms, her lush ass right in my face, her long legs
kicking, her small fists hitting my back.

She smells of roses and fear.

Wendy.

It's her. I got her, I... Brought her over. It's why I was in the
real world in the first place, so that's a fucking win. If only I
didn't hurt everywhere and if she stopped squirming...

Because dammit, my dick likes it way too much and my
head hurts too bad, and until I sort through my fucked-up
thoughts, I can't.

Can't fucking think.

I need to find the others.

Skirting the town, I head toward the hill rising over the
fields, keeping an eye out for mermaids despite the damn
exhaustion. It's swampy and they often come out of ponds, grab
your feet and try to drag you down with them.

Fucking island.

Fucking nightmare.

At some point, I realize she's stopped beating on my back
and I wonder if she's okay, if she's still breathing. If I should

care. But hell, after all the trouble I went through to get her, she'd better be.

Something slithers around my ankle, yanking, and I almost go down. Wendy smacks a small fist against the small of my back as I curse and grind my molars, pulling until my leg is freed.

Fucking dammit.

At least the girl is still alive.

I trudge up the hill, my breathing ragged, splinters of pain jamming into my sides. I spent too long in the real world and it fucked me up worse.

Fucking joy.

Still cursing under my breath, I limp toward home. Or whatever you call the half-buried dungeon where we currently live.

We actually call it the Foxhole, or just "the house", but it must have been an underground shelter at some point. An air-raid shelter?

Do you get air-raid shelters in nightmares?

Why the fuck not, right?

Dragging my feet for the last yard, staggering down the steps, I crow out our usual greeting—"Lost Boys!"—and kick the door open.

Only to find Tink in my face with his short sword in one hand and a grin on his face. He starts, "Peter, you fucker, the—"

"Move!" With a snarl, I shove his annoying ass out of the way and lurch the rest of the way inside to dump the girl on the ratty brown sofa. "Fuck."

"You're in a mood." Tink twirls the short sword cheerfully and whistles a little tune. "I'd say it's nice to have you back but you don't seem to think so."

"Shut up, Tink." I groan as I straighten. I reach for him without thinking, needing to touch him, reassure myself he's okay, feed the dark desire for him burning in my veins, but he somehow manages to move out of range before I do. "I'm getting too damn old for this."

"You're not old," he says.

Fuck, I hadn't realized I said that out loud.

"You don't get old," he goes on. "None of us do. Nightmares, see. That's their magic. They freeze horrible things in place."

Yeah, we are horrible things, but I don't feel like talking. I limp over to a chair and swallow another groan as I fall in it gracelessly.

My leg burns like the fires of hell.

"The Twins?" I ask.

"Out hunting. We weren't expecting you for dinner."

Ignoring the sarcasm that seems to lace every word Tink speaks, I close my eyes and breathe out, trying to get a grip on the pain, hoping nobody will talk to me for a while. Leave me in peace to rest.

But Tink wouldn't know the need for alone time if it bit him in his muscular ass. He ambles over and lifts the hem of my pants with the tip of his sword.

He tsks. "Mermaid venom?"

Moot question. He can see it with his own eyes. Where the mermaid's nails scratched me as I'd swum through the dark sea, carrying Wendy to shore, black tracks spread under my skin.

I don't even have the strength to reach for him this time, and he doesn't come any closer, either.

Same dance. Same story.

Wendy is making noises from the sofa—not the interesting kind, mind you, which would be sounds of pain or sex. She's more like... grumbling to herself as she attempts to straighten her soaked clothes that are already stiffening with salt, like mine.

It'd be cute if she wasn't yet another girl, yet another nuisance to put up with, with no real hope to offer.

A waste of my time.

"What is this place?" she mutters with a huff, finally sitting up, rubbing her palms over her thighs.

She's wearing woolen black stockings and a short skirt and low boots. Her sweater dips low enough that when she leans forward to rest her elbows on her knees, it affords me a nice view of her cleavage.

"Who are you?" she asks. "Why did you bring me here? Take me back."

I shift on the chair, my hard-on getting uncomfortable.

What the fuck is with this girl, this bedraggled, annoying chatterbox of a girl that gets me so hard when the previous ones were barely a blip on my radar?

"Oh. A girl!" Tink turns toward her, resting the sword on his shoulder, another manic grin on his face. "Damn, and I was sure it was a sack of potatoes. Such a pity. I miss potatoes."

There's a pause.

Her brows knit as she regards him for a long moment. "Are you a crazy person?" she asks calmly.

I laugh, a low chuckle that hurts my chest. Then again, everything hurts. "She sees right through you, Tink."

"I'm not mad," he growls, his grin vanishing in smoke. "Never say that."

Ow. Girl pushed a button. "This is Wendy," I say because that much I remember. As to why I brought her here...

"A Wendy." Tink relaxes. "Another one." He sniffs. "A pretty one. Is she the right one?"

"How the fuck should I know?" I grumble and run my gaze over him, the one I can't have, annoyed when my cock gets even harder, so damn hard it throbs like an open wound, a crazed animal trapped in the cage of my pants.

"She's too pretty to be the right one," Tink declares.

He's probably got a point. "Maybe."

"Don't talk about me as if I'm not here," she demands.

Tink laughs.

I snort.

Lord, she has a lot to learn.

"Maybe this time the magic will work." Tink turns back toward me, his grin returning, irrepressible. "Pretty or not, maybe she can do it."

"Magic?" She looks from him to me. "Are you serious? Is this an elaborate joke? Wait… Did Charlie put you up to it?"

I give her a blank look. Did I forget something here? Something more?

But Tink looks just as blank.

"Not a joke," Tink finally says. "Magic is real."

She huffs, almost laughs. They all do, at first. But the silence stretches, and her expression tightens.

"Look, I'm not a witch," she protests, "or whatever you think I am. I can't help you."

"We don't need a witch," I inform her. "We need a human."

"A human." She lifts her chin. "Then what would that make you?"

I shrug. "Inhuman. Monsters."

She shakes her head. Fear flashes in her eyes. "You really are mad." She turns to Tink. "You said, 'another Wendy.' Did you bring others to the island? Other girls, like me?"

"Oh yeah. Every ten years, Peter brings a Wendy here. But it's never been the right one."

"You do?" Now she turns to me, her eyes wide, her cheeks paling. "You regularly kidnap girls?"

"Not just *girls*," I say patiently, with more patience, in fact, than I feel. "Wendies."

"Whatever." She dismisses my clarification. "And how do you know they aren't the right ones?"

"They all went mad and jumped off the cliffs."

Now her face goes white as milk. "What did you just say? Jesus. Oh, sweet Jesus. This is it, I'm leaving." And she gets up, just like that, and heads toward the door, long blond hair flying.

I blink after her. What the fuck? She's not easily impressed, this one. Not even my growling and Tink's insane grin seem to faze her.

Or maybe they do and that's why she's running?

"You shouldn't run," Tink tells her, turning his head to follow her with his eyes.

"Watch me," she hisses, limping a little in her low boots. Did she hurt her foot coming out of the sea?

"There's no way off the island anyway," Tink says.

She grabs the door handle, turns it, and Tink still doesn't move to stop her.

I glare at him.

So I get up, hissing at the burn in my leg. Why the fuck is this all up to me? I can't even remember why she's here but I know I need to keep her around.

Fuck.

Limping worse than her, I make for the door, but she's already opened it and climbed up the steps, getting out and running away.

A roar rips out of my throat as I follow her out, my limp turning into an uneven loping run that eats the distance.

Fucking shit. My leg is on fire from the mermaid's venom, my head is pounding, my dick is rock-hard in my pants, and she *runs*?

"I don't get it," Tink mutters behind me. "Does she wanna die?"

Beats me.

She stands no fucking chance. I catch her before she even reaches the path, grab her arm and haul her back to the house —the bunker—as she yells at me to let go.

Before we get to the steps leading down to the door, I push her against the upper half of the outside wall that's protruding from the ground, face first, press my body to her back, and just breathe in her scent of soap and floral deodorant, of salt from the sea and sweet, aroused girl.

And those damn roses.

"Let me go!" She's squirming again, and damn, it's so fucking distracting. "I have a family! My brothers need me."

"Do I fucking look like I care?" I breathe in her ear and pull out one of my knives, the one I keep in my belt. I press it to her neck, run the flat of the cold blade over her unblemished skin. "Huh?"

"Oh, God..." She whimpers. Her throat clicks as she swallows. "Please, don't kill me..."

"Then stop running," I growl, caressing her skin with the blade. My dick is pressed against her ass, my arm wrapped around her waist, my breath is on her neck.

"I have to go back..."

"You're not going anywhere." Sheathing my knife, I lick her skin, salty and sweet, and lower my hand from her belly, dipping it under her skirt, into her panties. "Got it?"

Her breath goes out when I find her clit and circle it with my forefinger. That gets her attention alright.

"Please," she whispers.

She's soaked, and it would be so damn easy to lift her skirt and fuck her right here, against the wall.

So fucking easy.

But I swirl my finger again, pressing a little, and she moans. She's trembling, afraid and shocked, and yet aroused.

I feel a bitter chuckle rising in my throat. The dark and the fog have carried me here, and that same darkness lives inside of me, but to find her responding to it?

Hard to believe.

I press her harder against the half-buried wall until her cheek is mashed to its surface.

From the corner of my eye, I see Tink standing on the top step, arms folded over his chest, chewing on a grass stalk.

I see the Twins at the edge of the path, standing very still and watching intently.

Arousal flares, blasting through me. I want them to watch. I want her to squirm. Can she see them? Does she know we have an audience?

"Tinker," I say. "Colt. Wesson. Meet Wendy Darling."

She jerks a little, and I swirl my finger around her clit again, then slide it lower and push it into her hot pussy.

A cry escapes her as she comes on the spot, clenching around my finger, drenching her panties more.

Dammit. She *does* like this.

But soon she'll come down from her high, realize what happened and hate me for it. Fucking despise me.

Good.

It's what she's supposed to do. Loathe and abhor me. Hate my guts.

But let's be honest. Most probably, she already does.

4

WENDY

Whatʼs happening to me?

Stabbed, carried away, stranded with two madmen, and now strummed like an instrument in front of two more, inexplicably and painfully aroused, his knowing fingers pushing me over the edge so easily.

Fine, Iʼve only been with three guys total since I moved to town, but truth is, not one of them has managed to make me come.

And this Peter is a bastard. I shove back at him but he only chuckles low, a dark, delicious sound that makes me clench again.

"Let go!" I shove back again. "Damn you, let me go!"

Christ. Iʼm in shock, Iʼm most definitely in shock.

His hand withdraws from between my legs and his weight lifts off my back, but his long fingers close around my wrist and he hauls me behind him, back toward the house.

"This is a dream," I whisper, my voice breaking. Iʼm wet between my legs, and I can still feel his finger pushing into me. "Just a dream."

"This is real," he says, dragging me down the steps, pulling me inside and throwing me back on the sofa. "Though it's built from dreams."

Not sure how his words make any sense. "You said it's my dream earlier," I whisper.

Only one way to find out, right?

I pinch myself, as hard as I can.

And... *ouch*. I felt that. *Ow*. I rub at the reddened skin, still breathing hard from everything that happened—being hauled here, having Peter catch me and then bring me off so roughly against the wall, with everyone watching.

Oh God...

This isn't a dream, only it really looks like one. In fact, it looks...

I climb back to my feet, looking wildly around, even as the other guys come down into the underground house. I know... I know this place, too.

"Shit," I mutter. "Shit!"

"What?" It's the copper-head, the crazy one with the short sword, who enters first, his worn gray jeans hanging low on his narrow hips, his scuffed army boots thumping on the floor. His t-shirt is a soft blue and clings to his ripped chest distractingly. "Who shit in our house?"

I roll my eyes at him. "This place feels familiar."

"Oh, stop worrying your head over that or you'll go mad, too." He grins as he stalks over to me and stops in front of me. "Hi. Name's Tink. Tink Bell."

"Wendy," I say automatically, caught short by his looks. "Wendy Darling."

"A Darling Wendy." He grins wider, that manic glint showing again in his eyes—and what eyes they are. A deep green, bottle-green, but calling them that wouldn't do them justice. They're gorgeous, bright and fringed with long lashes.

And his hair... It's a light copper with pink streaks. Interesting choice.

But it's not just the colors, it's the shapes that turn him into a kind of forest god—that shapely mouth, always talking and grinning, those high cheekbones, that square jaw, those dimples in his cheeks.

I'm staring and I can't stop. I can't help myself, he's so *pretty*.

One of the twins comes to shove him aside—they have to be twins because their strong bodies and handsome faces are copies of each other, though their colors are strangely reversed —and he shoves right back with a snarl, his grin vanishing.

"Wait for your turn, Wes."

"You were taking way too fucking long," Wes snarls right back, and I find myself gaping at him.

At both twins.

Definitely mirror images of each other, they're both tall and strong, more whipcord than muscular, leaner than Peter, and yet with shoulders broader than Tink's. They both have gorgeous faces with Roman noses and hard jaws, eyes like fire.

But Wes, the one growling at Tink right now, has short blond hair, longer bangs falling in eyes like old gold.

Whereas his brother who's standing behind him, strong arms crossed over his chest and a sardonic smile on his lips, has long dark hair pulled back in a man-bun and dark eyes that glint dangerously.

And then it hits me again that these guys, all these handsome, strange men, they were there as Peter pressed me to the wall and got me off.

Did I moan loud enough to be heard?

Did they realize what was happening?

Of course they did. Now my face is burning. My chest feels too tight.

The dark twin advances on me, grabs my wrist before I can flee—though, where, I don't know—and hauls me against his tall, hard body.

"A Wendy," he says with a half-smile curling up one side of

his mouth. A strand of hair has escaped his bun and clings to his strong jaw, his long neck.

"Wendy Darling," his brother provides, returning my attention to him. "Fitting, right, Colt?"

Colt, then, is the dark one's name. His smile spreads. "A Darling, huh?"

I pull my hand away but his grip only tightens. "Who are you guys?" I whisper. "What is this place?"

"Didn't Pan tell you? This is Neverland."

"Never heard of such a place."

"It doesn't exist in time," Colt says. "*Never*, got it? A place outside of time."

I shake my head. "You're crazy. All of you. I'm going home."

This time when I yank my hand away, Colt releases me and I stumble around him, around them, heading once more toward the door.

Peter makes a low growling sound in his throat, like an animal. "What did I say?" His voice comes distorted to my ears as I open the door once more. "What did I say about running away? Tink. Get her."

I barely manage a step outside, when a whirlwind catches me and hauls me back inside, slamming me down onto the frigging sofa and caging me with his arms.

Tink. That's who the whirlwind is.

Gone is the prettiness and playfulness from his face, replaced by an ugly sneer, a fanged mouth and... are those wings rising over his shoulders?

Gossamer, I think, stunned, *taut blue silk with purple and golden veins.*

Like an evil fairy, a goblin of myth, a delicate gargoyle about to tear me to shreds.

Oh God, this is it. It's done. I've gone off the deep end.

"Caught," he breathes and licks his lips, his eyes gone slitted and dark, his ears twitching—pointed and sort of tufted. He arches like a big cat, then presses down, grinding his body on top of mine, a hard rod of arousal rubbing over my belly, up, between my breasts. "Caught, my Darling. Oh, yeah."

Panting, I manage to move, placing my hands on his chest and pushing—but his chest is hard like a wall of stone under my palms, hard planes of muscles curving under the worn fabric, and my fingers helplessly follow them.

Then he distracts me more. He lowers himself until his hard-on presses right between my legs and it feels so good, I moan.

Caught, like he said.

Caught in the moment, in the pleasure, in the feel of this inhumanly beautiful man on top of me, his aura of danger and magic slamming into me, making my nipples stiff and my belly clench.

Even the pink streaks in his hair have turned to black, I realize. He bends his head over mine and he licks at my lips, a rough swipe, a groan escaping him.

"She tastes good," he rumbles, "Peter, listen, I think—"

A force lifts him off me and sends him flying, crashing into the far wall.

I scream, sitting up, flailing as I try to move away, not sure where I could go.

Then I glance at Tink and I scream again because he's sprawled on his back on the floor, face rolled to the side and his eyes wide open, unblinking, staring right at me.

"Is he dead?" I breathe. "Did you kill him? Oh, my God, you killed him!"

"He doesn't get to touch you without my say-so," Peter growls. He's standing there, looking more like an animal than a man, teeth bared, tattooed hands clenched into fists, eyes flashing, more wolf-like than ever. I swear his canines are too sharp for a human.

Then again, these guys aren't human, are they? It's starting to dawn on me that wherever I am, it isn't in my world. I'm in frigging deep trouble.

"You killed him," I whisper.

"Did I?"

I glance again at Tink and start when I notice his hand twitch. Then I realize that his eyes have closed and his chest seems to be rising and falling.

Oh, thank God. I slump back in relief.

Though, why should I care if they kill each other? I shouldn't. I can't. It doesn't matter where I am or why. I need to find someone who will help me get away.

There's that ruined town we passed by. I just need to sneak out when they are asleep—assuming they sleep—and find a person who will tell me how to get back home.

5

TINK

U *ngh.* Who dropped a fucking three-story house on my head? Or was it a bridge? A tower?

Fucking hurts.

I'm jostled around and the pain sends flashes of light behind my eyes. I fight whoever's got his paws on me, but all I get is a freefall and crash-landing on... a soft surface.

It bounces.

A bed. *Oh, fuck.* I don't fucking like beds. They are omens of bad, bad things.

On cue, a slap to my cheek snaps my head to the side, and fucking *ow.* "What?" I demand, my voice coming our slurred. "Fuck."

"Rise and shine, Tinker," a familiar voice says and I blink at an upside-down face. It's familiar, too, to suit the voice.

I groan. "Get out of my sight, Wes."

"He's all right," Wes gives his diagnosis, disappearing from view. "Bastard halfling is hard to kill."

"Not that Peter doesn't try often enough lately," Colt replies.

The Twins.

I'm still trying to figure out whether standing up is a good idea and they are making out, obviously not overly concerned about me. Colt has his hands in Wes' short blond hair and is eating out his mouth hungrily. Wes is giving back as good as he gets, growling as he grips Colt's shoulders, kissing him hard, pressing him against the wall.

Sexy assholes.

They keep dragging me over to join them. As if that will ever happen.

Rolling on my side, I make an attempt at sitting and the second time, I manage it. With a groan, I pinch the bridge of my nose. "The fuck. Peter tried to kill me again?"

"His patience is on its last legs," Wes says.

They have stopped kissing, and now Wes is leaning against the bedroom wall, arms folded over his chest, a smirk on his stupid face. Colt stands beside him, one hand braced on the wall, his dark gaze on Wes as if he's about to turn him around and fuck him right now.

It wouldn't be the first time they quit a conversation to fuck.

"You've been saying that for decades." I rub at the back of my skull. Everything hurts.

"And you're getting more annoying by the day."

I let my hand drop. Rubbing isn't helping, anyway. "Well, thanks, asshole. What happened to accepting people as they are?"

He shrugs. "That works, unless they are annoying dipshits like you."

"I was only doing his bidding. 'Tink, go after her. Tink, bring her back.' I brought her back and what do I get in thanks?" I lift my hand and uncurl my middle finger in Peter's general direction. "Thrown against the wall, getting my brain rattled, that's what."

"To be fair, there isn't much brain in there to rattle," Colt points out and I resist the urge to punch him because, ow, head hurts, and I need to sit still for a while.

"Fuck you," I mutter, just to let him know how much I don't appreciate the comment.

"Come on, Tink. You were making out with her," Wes says, shifting so that his hip is pressed to Colt's. "What did you expect?"

"Bullshit. You call that making out? I only held her down."

Wes grins. "And she liked it."

I roll my eyes. "Not my fault she did, is it?"

"You liked it, too."

"That..." I shake my head. "It's the goddamn truth."

"And you knew Peter would get pissed," Wes goes on.

Fuck, my head... "I can't always guess what will set Peter off, okay? He's pissed all the goddamn time."

"Point," Colt concedes.

"Shut up," Wes mutters. "He might hear you. Or do you wanna feel his wrath, too?"

"This isn't okay," I breathe, tucking my hair behind my ears. "We joined him voluntarily and now he's acting like a dictator."

"Nothing is okay," Wes says, "if it has escaped your attention. He's been getting worse. Unstable. His magic is leaking all over the place."

"Doesn't mean it's all right," I grumble.

"And what would you have us do instead?" Colt demands, dark eyes flashing. "Abandon him? Abandon the island?"

"Too late for that," Wes says, sliding a hand around Colt's neck, tugging his head back. Colt groans softly. "There's no way back, Tink, and you know it. We stick together."

"She's not the right Wendy," I say.

They exchange quick looks.

"We don't know that," Wes says.

"The hell we don't. Where is her magic, huh? How is she going to break the dark curse?"

"None of the Wendies showed any sign of magic at first," Colt argues.

"Or later," I mutter. "Because they never had any."

"But the whole point is that they have to be human," he insists.

"Meaning, from the human world, you idjit." I sigh. "Not that they have to be magicless humans. How else are they supposed to do this, how are they going to help us, if not with magic?"

"We aren't supposed to know, Tink. Only keep searching, keep trying to fix the bridge."

With another groan, I swing my legs off the bed and manage not to roll my eyes, cuz, headache. "Yeah, yeah. We keep telling ourselves that. That there is a solution. That the Mermaid Queen knows something and we will find it out. That the Dark Fae King will let us go if we break this spell. That a human girl can do it. Well, guess what. For centuries it hasn't worked. No reason why it should work now. We're stuck, guys. Stuck on the other side."

"Which is technically your side," Colt says. "The Fae side."

"Shut up, Colt." I sigh, rub at my eyes. "Damn. We have to talk to Peter."

———

PETER IS ASLEEP IN ONE OF THE ARMCHAIRS WHEN WE RETURN TO the sitting room, his dark hair sticking up in all directions, an inked arm thrown over his face.

And so is Wendy, fast asleep, though she's curled up on the sofa, her blond hair draped over her face and her skirt riding dangerously high over her ass.

A nice handful of an ass.

Heart-shaped.

Lush.

My lip curls.

I don't touch her, though, ignoring my hard dick, and

instead head over to our wretched king. I grab him, tuning out the cursing of the Twins, and haul him to his feet, drag him to the wall and slam him against it, just like he did.

"Wakey, wakey," I growl and enjoy the flash of a shadow I see passing behind his eyes. "Are you with us now?"

"Tink," he growls back as his brain catches up. "What the fuck?"

"You forget that I'm not your plaything, *King*."

"Plaything? What the hell, man?" He shoves at me, and my anger bleeds out as realization hits me.

"You forgot again," I sigh.

"Forgot what?"

Taking a step back, I release him and glance over my shoulder at the Twins. They wear matching scowls on their faces, but I don't know if it's because I decided to go crazy and challenge Peter, or if it's because he's forgetting stuff again.

I mean, it's nothing new, this forgetfulness of his. Been happening for a long time now. Getting worse, though, *oh yeah*. Definitely.

Wes draws out his gun, twirls it on a finger. "Hey, Peter. Do you know where you are?"

"Are you fucking with me?" His pale eyes flick to where the Twins are standing. "I'm on the island."

We all sag a little in relief.

"But who's her?" he says, nodding at the sofa. "What is she doing here?"

Oh, fuck.

"Peter..." I start.

"Dammit," Colt breathes.

Wendy stirs, probably woken by our voices, and sits up, rubbing at her eyes. Then she blinks those big baby blues at us and says, "Hey, what did I miss?

6

WENDY

I dreamed I was home, shadows lurking in the corners, my brothers crying somewhere unseen, a cold dread in my stomach.

But that's the only thing I remember as I sit upright, brought to wakefulness by loud voices that don't quite fit in my dream.

Where...? *Oh. Right.*

The Mad World.

Neverland.

An island. Or a nightmare, inhabited by four gorgeous, crazy boys.

And it's all real.

Figures that I'd end up in such a place. Maybe I hit my head and I'm in a coma. Or maybe this is the real world but it's an asylum for the mentally challenged.

I open my mouth to suggest my newest theory—maybe this island is a rock in the sea like Alcatraz but for crazies—when I realize they're all staring at me.

Tink, Colt and Wes are *glaring* at me, in fact, for some unfathomable reason, and it's scary.

But what sends a chill down my spine is the look in Peter's eyes.

It's one of blank confusion.

"What's going on?" I whisper, glancing at the others and back at him. "You're scaring me."

Last thing I remember was the Twins carrying Tink out of the room and Peter sitting in the armchair, a scowl on his handsome face, toying with his knife.

Now he's looking at me as if he doesn't know who or *what* I am.

He takes a step toward me, lifting his hand as if to touch, as if disbelieving his eyes, but he falters. His knees go out from under him and he goes down.

Before he hits the ground, though, Tink steps in and grabs him under the arms in a move that looks practiced. "Peter. Easy now." Holding him up with impossible strength, he drags him back toward the armchair. "Come on."

It's my turn to stare in incomprehension. "What's wrong with him?"

"Him? Oh." Tink sits Peter on the armchair, Colt joining him to settle Peter on the cushions. "Nothing. It's just... He gets flashes."

I stare. "Flashes of what?"

"The past? The future? Other planets? Who knows?"

I shake my head. "You're not making any sense. And why are you helping him? He tried to kill you."

"I know." Tink suddenly grins, straightening, patting Peter's shoulder. "He's been trying for a long time now. Man doesn't know when to give up."

"You are all so strange," I whisper and good God, I mean it.

"Right. We know." Wes holsters his gun. He has a belt holster at his hip like he's a cowboy or something.

Colt lifts a dark brow.

Peter is rubbing his eyes with his fists. "Goddamn headache," he mutters.

"It's a little problem he has." Tink taps his own temple. "Right here. Leaky memory."

"Shut up, Tink," Peter grunts, grimacing. He really seems to be in pain.

A part of me feels sorry for him, but the memory of how he hauled me here, of how he pressed me to the wall and got me off in front of everyone—of how he tried to kill Tink...

No pity, I tell myself. *He doesn't deserve it. What am I even thinking? Falling asleep with these guys around, letting my guard down? You'd think that growing up the way I did, I'd know better.*

It's quiet, I realize. They are looking at me as if waiting for something.

I scowl back at them. Eye the door. Grind my molars. I need to be compliant, make them lower their guard, too. That will be my chance to run.

So I bow my head and force my jaw to relax. "I'm hungry," I say.

The silence twangs like a chord. Their brows start climbing up their foreheads.

"She's hungry," Colt says after a long moment.

"Of course she's hungry," Wes says. "Peter grabbed her hours ago."

"A day ago," Tink says.

A day ago. *Jesus.* What will Charlie think? She'll be so worried.

But Peter pushes to his feet before I have the chance to work myself into a panic, dark hair bristling, dark tattoos seeming to writhe on his pale skin, and I remember I need to worry about myself more right now.

"Come on," Colt says, gesturing toward the back of the room where an arched doorway is half-open. How didn't I notice it before? "Let's grab some dinner."

"I'm not cooking," Tink declares, as if he's expected to, and I realize another thing: his wings are gone.

He had wings last time I saw him, right? And sharp teeth? Why does he look like a normal, gorgeous guy now?

"Whatever," Peter grumbles, advancing on me.

I take a step back. "What do you want?"

"You're coming with us." He grabs my wrist and pulls. "Come on."

"Ow. Let go."

He doesn't. Instead, he drags me toward the arched door. "Can you cook?"

The only thing I can cook is omelets but I don't say that. "I'm not your mother," I mutter.

"Oh, I know that," he says bitterly. "She was a junkie and she's been dead for a long time now."

Oh.

"Depression is a bitch," Wes says with a shrug, pushing the arched door open all the way for Peter to drag me through, not making a move to help me, the bastard. "She overdosed. Then of course his demented uncle took him in, and when he ran, he ran to the Dark Fae. Hardly an improvement."

"Jesus," I breathe.

"It was long ago, like I said," Peter mutters darkly, pulling me into a large space with a table and chairs and... a fireplace? "I don't remember her."

"Course not. Duh. You were little. And you tend to forget things." Wes clucks his tongue as he stalks inside and heads straight for the fireplace. "Guess it's up to me to cook again."

"Again?" Peter scowls. "What do you mean, again?"

"Peter, my man, I know your memory is going, but Colt and I have been keeping you fed for the past century. Try to keep up."

Peter scowls. "Damn."

"Let go," I mutter and try to pull my wrist away, free it from

Peter's grip. "Why do you keep grabbing me and dragging me around? I'm not your slave."

"Feisty, this one," Wes says, running his fingers through his short blond hair, through the spikes in the front. "Fun."

"Screw you," I hiss. "All of you. What's this, a cult of some sort? A mafia gang thing? Are you serial killers, hiding in the wilderness?"

And yeah, I know I told myself to keep a low profile, not upset them, but seriously? Screw these guys.

"Okay," Tink says, giving me a narrow look, "did you miss the magical part?"

"I guess I have," I mutter sullenly.

"Then let me demonstrate," he says and opens his arms.

"Tink!" Colt has a frown on his face. "Stop showing off."

Tink shrugs. "She has to see to believe."

"See what?" I mutter.

Light sparkles in front of him, bubbles of brightness rising as if through liquid to slowly spin around his head, reflected in his eyes.

Those beautiful wings from before spring out of his back, trembling and shedding sparks of white light, and behind him... behind him, I think I see white towers and black trees and great winged creatures flying against a dark sky.

Whoa.

I take a step back only to be brought short by Peter's relentless grip on my wrist.

"Where are you going?" he demands, brow furrowed.

"That's... magic." I know I sound stupid but I can't help it. It's magic. Or is it a trick? Is he... an illusionist? Yeah, maybe that's it, he's making me think that he—

"It *is* magic, yeah," Peter says flatly. "We call him Tinker because he tinkers with reality."

"But... magic." I swallow hard. "Like... it's not an illusion? Can he really, I don't know... change reality?"

"It's not that simple," Peter says. "Or that complicated. There are other layers of reality, different ones. And he can make the boundary between the two vanish."

"Like...?" I try to think of fantasy movies I've watched. "Like open a portal?"

"No. No portals," Peter says. "He avoids breaking through to the other side. Mostly."

"Why...?" I swallow all my inane questions. "Wait, how do you know all this? Can you all do magic?"

"We have our gifts," Wes says cryptically, coming to stand beside me as Tink continues to play with the lights. "Each magic is different."

"Let me help you express yourself. My magic is better, is what you're trying to say," Tink says, his voice chiming like bells all around us. His wings tremble, shed drops of light. "Tink Bell the Fae Mongrel at your service."

"Show-off," Colt says again.

"Fuck off," Tink says, shooting him a sweet smile. "Convinced yet, Wendy?"

"Turn off your fairy lights and conjure up some food, will ya?" Colt grumbles.

I'm still gaping at Tink when the floating lights around him wink out and the other world visible behind him vanishes.

He huffs. "You know as well as I, Colt, that I won't be stealing food from the Fae just to fill your stomach and give our location up."

"Goddammit, stop bickering and arguing, all of you!" Peter roars and hauls me closer, against his side. I don't resist, partly in shock, partly because... it feels good to be held at his side, my boob pressed to his muscle-wrapped ribcage, his powerful arm coming around my back to keep me in place.

Instinctively, I raise my arms and wrap them around him, too, and he smells... delicious.

Somehow already familiar.

Sexy.

With a sigh, Colt lifts a basket and slams it on top of the narrow counter running along the wall by the fireplace. "We'll have the usual fare then."

"Yum." Tink bares those disconcertingly sharp fangs that remind me... of bad things from my nightmares.

Then again, what nightmares are ever good, right?

7

WENDY

The Twins are cooking.

Meanwhile, Tink has sprawled in a chair by the long, scratched table, examining his nails.

And Peter and I are still standing there, in a frozen tableau.

To be honest, I don't want to move, even though his stillness is a bit unnerving. His heart is beating steadily under my ear that's pressed to his hard pec, a strong, reassuring rhythm.

There's something... *off* about Peter.

Off, and at the same time alluring. I think about it as Colt chops various veggies and Wes butchers a small animal on a board. The smell of blood invades my senses, but I try to ignore it.

I'd rather think about Peter's otherness.

For instance, Tink is dressed in casual clothes, the Twins wear a darker palette—dark pants and shirts—but Peter...

Peter isn't dressed in modern clothes, I realize, and there's something about a guy with full sleeves of ink and old-fashioned clothes.

Since he brought me to the island, he's changed out of his filthy, ripped black hoodie. Now he's wearing a white button-down shirt with a pocket over his heart, and his slacks seem tailored. Even his shoes from what I can see look old style—narrow, shiny, laced up, with a heel.

His dark hair is tousled, but he has a parting on one side, like an old picture in a frame.

Who is he?

Who are they all and how did they end up here?

The asylum theory is still my preferred one, but it doesn't add up. They have guns and knives and... where are the guards and nurses and doctors?

I mean... probably these men escaped from the asylum and are hiding in the woods or something. *Right?*

Yeah, that makes so much sense.

Uh. Sort of.

Still doesn't help me understand any of it. I don't know of any asylums, or beaches for that matter, near where I live. And it doesn't explain why this place looks like something from my nightmares, or how Tink can make lights dance and project another world behind him.

Explanations abound, I remind myself. *No matter what Peter said, it's all illusions. And as for this place feeling familiar... you see what you want to see. You convinced yourself that this place is familiar when in fact it's just the dark atmosphere and the fear gripping you that makes you think that.*

Right.

"What the fuck?" Peter suddenly says, pulling me from my thoughts. He's staring down at me, brows drawn together. "Who are you?"

I stare back at him, a continuous 'what the fuck' going through my head. "What?"

"Ah, for fuck's sake, Peter." Tink gets up from the chair and comes to put a hand on Peter's shoulder. "It's all right, man. It's Wendy. You brought her over today."

Peter lets out a long breath, though his jaw is still locked tight with suspicion. "I did? Fuck. Okay."

"You should eat something," Tink goes on. "It always helps restart your brain."

"What would you know about it?" Peter mutters.

Now I'm trying to pull away but he won't let me. What's up with him and always holding on to me, huh? "Peter..."

"It's okay. Fuck, fuck." His arm around my back is like a band of steel. "Sit."

"Stop ordering me about!"

With a soft curse, he drags me to the table and plops me down in a chair. "Stay," he hisses and stalks out of the room, slamming the door shut behind him.

"What was that about" I whisper, scared and yet not scared enough. I'm more... sad, I realize. Why am I sad? "What's wrong with him?"

"Oh, Peter is..." Tink whistles, twirls his finger at his temple. "Not all there. Like you said earlier."

"Crazy?" I breathe.

"Away with the fairies," Tink says. "I mean, he's definitely got a few loose screws. Ah... It's the dust he snorts. And also his wound."

I glance the way Peter went. "What wound?"

"His shadow is detached. Torn. It doesn't fully fit him anymore."

"What does that even mean?" I demand.

"It's a long story."

"Do I look like I got anything else to do?" I bite out. "Or that I'm allowed to go anywhere?"

"Good point." Tink glances at the closed door, too, then sits down next to me. God, he's beautiful. Peter's beauty is savage, hard, but Tink's is just... mesmerizing, and his scent wafts over me, wild and peppery with a hint of flowers. "But I can't discuss this."

"Discuss what?" I snap. "Yourself? This insane situation? Kidnapping me?"

"Whoa. Kidnapping is a strong word."

I put my hands on my hips. "It's an accurate word."

Colt snorts. "She has you there, Tinkers."

"Keep cooking, Colton," Tink growls.

That distracts me. "His name is Colton?"

"Nah. But it annoys him when I call him that. He's named Colt, after the gun. So, Wendy..." Tink tilts his head and gives me that crooked grin that makes my heart skip a beat. He has his hair tucked behind an ear and... okay, am I seeing things?

I reach out without thinking and touch his slightly pointed ear. "Oh, my God."

"Oh. Shit." He jerks back, the legs of his chair screeching. "No touching without a warning, girl."

"Sorry."

"It's okay. Fuck." He's breathing hard. His hair has fallen over his ears again, hiding them and his face looks pale. "Just... don't."

"See, Tink's got issues, too." Wes dumps the meat he's cut up into a pan where it sizzles. "Don't you, Tink?"

"We all do," Tink grinds out.

Yeah, that makes sense.

"Did you... run away from a madhouse?" I blurt out, then press my back into my chair as Tink's eyes widen, then harden.

He lets out a harsh laugh. "You could say that."

"Again with the riddles," I complain. "What do you mean?"

"It was easier in the past, you know." He tsks.

"What was easier?"

"People believed in fairies. In magic. In the Otherworld. One didn't have to explain anything."

"Boo," I whisper. "I feel for you."

He stares at me, then another harsh bark of laughter escapes him. "Damn."

"We didn't run away from a madhouse, Darling," Wes says, turning to face me, propping a hip against the counter, folding his arms, bloody hands and all. His grin is sharp like a blade. "But these guys? Tink and Peter? They should have been locked up, the key thrown away."

"Oh, really." Tink snorts.

"As for Colt and me?" Wes shrugs. "We are the only sane ones on this island."

"So he says," Tink mutters.

"Unless there's a fight," Colt says.

"Oh, yeah." Wes nods. "Unless there's a fight. Then we go nuts."

"We go off," Colt snickers. "Get it? Like guns."

So reassuring... *not.* "A fight? With whom?"

"Ah. That's the part we can't tell you about," Tink says.

"Why the hell not? You brought me here!" I slap the top of the table, frustration winning over my fear. I'm losing it. "Why? What do you want from me? Is it ransom? I have to tell you, my parents are broke and not only that, I bet they don't give a damn whether I live or die, so you're out of luck!"

They're all staring at me again.

Eventually, Wes sighs and turns back to his veggies. "Out of luck. You could say that. Been out of luck for centuries now. Let's just eat."

———

THE VEGETABLES ARE FRESH AND CRISPY—A SORT OF SALAD I can't identify, and the meat is soft and gamey. Holding it with my fingers, I tear into it with my teeth, suddenly famished.

"Good, huh?" Wes is watching me intently, licking his lips as I chew and swallow, his golden eyes darkening, focused on my mouth. "Mm..."

"Delicious," Colt says, and he isn't eating, either, just

watching me. His cheekbones are flushed, making his dark eyes shine.

"It is," I admit, and grab another piece of meat. "Won't you eat?"

"I'd rather... let you have it," Colt says, his voice a little hoarse. "You're hungry."

Their gazes locked on me are hungry, too. When I turn to Tink, I find him leaning back in his chair, his hand moving between his legs.

"What are you doing?" I demand.

"Enjoying." He grins. "Don't mind me."

He's jacking off. At the table. Beside me.

Christ.

It's hot. He's hot. Why is it so hot? Shouldn't this bother me, like, really bother me that these pervs are beating their meat as they watch me eat?

What's the matter with me?

Distracted, I chew more slowly—and then bite down on something hard.

"Ow." I spit it out. "What's this? A frigging *bullet*?"

Colt shrugs. "Should have warned ya. Sorry." He pats his gun at his side. "We hunt with what we got."

"You shot a hare with your gun?"

He frowns. "Is that worse than catching it in a snare? It was a quick death, I promise."

I push my plate away, my stomach churning.

I mean, look, I'm not a squeamish eater and I'm aware that all meat comes from living animals, and it's not even that. It's not even the bullet.

It's the reminder yet again of where I am, and with whom.

"Just explain why you can't tell me anything," I whisper. "I can't... can't pretend that everything's okay."

"Everything's definitely not okay," Tink says, still stroking himself, eyes half-closed. "And Peter has watched you for years and years. Lucky voyeuristic bastard, if only he wasn't losing his mind. We only get to watch you now for the first time. Have a heart."

One word catches my full attention. "For *years*? What do you mean?"

"Stop talking, Tink," Colt snaps and gets up, stalking around the table toward me. "We can't fucking tell you why you're here, Wendy, because if we do, Hook will hear it."

"Hook? Who's that?" I glance at the others. "And how will he hear us?"

"Goddammit." Colt grabs me, lifting me up and slinging me over his shoulder as if I weigh no more than a frigging raincoat. "I said it's not safe."

"No!" I fight him as best I can, but he's pure muscle and doesn't even seem to notice. "Put me down. I just ate, I'll throw up!"

"Don't you fucking dare," he mutters as he strides out of the room. "If you puke on me, I'll spank you. Maybe I'll spank you anyway."

"No! What the hell?" I hit his back with my fists but he doesn't seem to feel a thing. Turning my head, I see Wes and Tink are following us, smirking. "Put me down!"

"Stop making so much noise," Colt snaps.

The others' smirks widen.

"What are you all smiling for?" I yell. "You're all psychos!"

"That's too much noise," Wes says.

"Way too much," Tink agrees.

I'm so mystified, I stop struggling. "What are they talking about?"

Colt carries me into another room, a much darker one, and fear closes around my heart again. He dumps me on a surface and a scream almost bursts out of me as I fall, before I register that it's a bed.

Hard as hell but a bed nevertheless, the feeling of falling caught by the mattress.

Then Colt is on top of me—much like Tink was earlier today on the sofa—and his mouth closes over mine, sealing my lips, taking my breath.

I squirm on the bed, startled and unsure, everything happening too fast—but as Colt's body presses down on mine, I relax.

He's warm, so warm, and heavy, all muscle. His taste is smokey and briny and sweet, like salty caramel, his stubble scraping against my chin. His dark hair has come loose from its bun, framing his face, and my fingers tangle in it.

God, he tastes good, feels even better. His eyes are almost closed, long dark lashes fanning over his cheekbones, his cheeks lean, his jaw so sharp you could cut diamonds on it. I trace it with my fingertips as he kisses me, my thoughts turning into a twisted knot inside my head.

My body, though... My body likes this way too much. It had wanted Colt from the moment I saw him, wanted all these gorgeous, mysterious guys, and although my mind is in shock, my body is just in lust.

"Move over, brother," Wes says then, and suddenly he's claiming my mouth upside down, seated behind my head, his hand gripping my chin, pushing his brother back with the other.

I gasp into his mouth, the new angle making me arch up against his brother who curses loudly, moaning as his hard length presses between my legs where I'm starting to ache with need.

Wes's tongue pushes into my mouth, stroking, as his firm lips move over mine, his taste different, a brighter echo of his brother's, his scent slightly bitter but also salty and spicy.

God...

"Goddammit," Tink hisses, and comes to stand beside the

bed, his hand inside his pants, stroking furiously. "Goddamn Twins. Peter will be so damn mad. Oh, I like it."

I'm kissing Wes back, still arching up and rubbing myself shamelessly against Colt's strong, aroused body, against his hard-on, Tink's words adding fuel to the fire raging inside me.

I've never felt so out of control, so out of caution. Since the boating incident, I've been a good girl, careful, quiet, serious, all about taking care of my brothers and getting us all out of that house, but now...

Now it's as if I've thrown all caution to the wind, as if my control has snapped for the first time in ten years, as if the shock of this abduction and the craziness of the situation has driven me wild.

I need.

I'm so aroused I hurt.

I want their hands and mouths on me, I want their cocks in me, I want to be untethered and allowed to fly.

Colt is still cursing, reaching between us to unzip his pants, Tink is panting, the wide head of his cock protruding over his unbuttoned jeans, Wes is kissing me like he wants to eat me up, and—

"What the fuck?" Peter is at the door, his expression stormy. "You fucking fools. Hook is on his way."

8

COLT

Oh-uh. Peter is pissed off.

Then again, his moods have always been mercurial, and have gotten worse over the past few years.

It's as if he can feel his time running out, flowing through his fingers, vanishing into the void.

And then... wait, *what*?

"*Hook*? Coming *here*? What the fuck are you saying?" I yank myself off Wendy and adjust my hard-on inside my pants. "That's bullshit."

"He heard you, goddammit, going at it like fucking rabbits." Peter gets in my face, eyes narrow and teeth bared. "You know he can sense it when we fuck her."

"Hey." I back away, lifting my hands. Peter's anger can be formidable, and so is his power. He is the king, after all. "All we did was kiss."

"And some of us didn't even get to that," Tink grumbles, "and still got punished. Remember throwing me against the wall? Remember—?"

"She doesn't belong to you, Peter," I mutter.

"What was that?" Peter's attention returns to me.

"You did get her off outside when she first arrived. I thought you didn't care if Hook knew. All I'm saying is..." I lift my shoulders in a shrug. "She's not the one, man. We talked about it."

"Fuck." He runs a hand through his hair. "We did? Well, it doesn't matter. Hook now he thinks she's the one and he'll come to take her."

"Take me?" Wendy has sat up and is tugging down her short skirt. Her face is red. "Take me where? Who is this Hook?"

"Hook used to be one of us," Wes says. "But he has fallen from grace."

"Shut up, Wes," Peter growls.

"Why? It's no big secret, even if he's still listening in."

Wendy gets up, and fuck, she's so short and slight and delicate in the center of the four of us I can't look away. "How can Hook listen in?"

"Like Tink, he's got magic," Peter says. "Unlike Tink, he's allied himself with the merfolk centuries ago, becoming somewhat merfolk himself, and therefore every liquid is an echoing chamber for him."

"Merfolk." She blinks those huge eyes. "And what did you say about Tink?"

"Tink's is half-Fae. Folk of the earth, I believe?"

"Earthen-were." Tink winks. "I'm actually Night Court."

"And the liquid that allowed Hook to listen in?" Wendy asks. "Where was the liquid?"

"There's a leak inside the bedroom," Wes says with a scowl. "Yeah, it's a literal leak. Of water."

"But also of information apparently," Peter says.

"I didn't think of that."

"Yeah," Peter says, "you didn't."

"How is that possible? A leak of water... merfolk and earth-Fae..." Wendy huffs. "Peter, you have to tell me what I'm doing here."

"Apart from fucking them?" he snarls.

"For your information," she steps right into his space, hands balled at her sides, a small volcano of rage to match his own, "you are the only one who actually put his hands inside my panties and put on a show for them, but now you have the gall to complain because they kissed me? For real?"

He blinks. Glances sideways at me as if asking for help and I almost laugh because this is a first.

Thing is, I don't know if he forgot about that little stunt of his earlier on, or if he's just out of his depth with a woman who talks back.

"I'm the King," he ends up saying.

"And I'm the Queen of Sheba."

He blinks. "Are you?"

"What are you, stupid? Oh, right," she waves a hand about, "this is an island out of time where you fight pirates and... and mermaids." Her face pales. "Shit, that mermaid was real, too, wasn't it?"

"Would I be limping if not?" he mutters, frowning.

He's annoyed.

Well, he's not the only one.

And wait, what the fuck?

"Peter!" I bark, "did the mermaid touch you?"

He looks down and blood is seeping through his pants. "Not much."

"Not much? That's venom!" I snap.

"I know what it is, Colt," Peter says. "My mind isn't all gone."

Yet. Not all gone *yet.* He doesn't say the word but it hangs in the air between us.

"So what's the cure for this venom?" Wendy asks, staring down at Peter's leg.

"I'm fine," he says and predictably grabs her wrist. Man's got a thing for control and... maybe touch? He rarely touches us anymore, too lost inside his head, his shadow moving him like a puppet, but he can't seem to stop touching Wendy. "Come on."

She shoots me a questioning look and I just shrug. If she's wondering about Peter, well, tough. Only he can tell her more, *if* he remembers.

And if she's worried about Hook arriving, she'll just have to join the club.

———

"W<small>HERE ARE WE GOING</small>?" <small>SHE ASKS AS WE FILE OUT OF THE HOUSE</small> and move among the trees, glancing back at us as Peter drags her along to his much wider strides.

"Leading Hook away from home," Tink says.

"Quiet," Peter snaps.

"What does it matter?" Tink makes a face. "It's the four of us, and Wendy. He has the numbers on his side."

"Numbers?" Wendy whispers. "Meaning?"

"Hook took the Dark Fae side. He fights for the coalition of the Unseelie Fae and the merfolk. Goddamn pirate."

She stumbles, curses, glances back again. "So what, he's got an army?"

"Of sorts."

"And what are we gonna do?"

She says "we" like it's decided, like she's the one we need, like she doesn't hate us, like we're a team.

Peter doesn't seem to notice. "Wes, you take her and hide her. Meet you back at the house when the moon sets."

"Why Wes?" I demand, caught off guard. Usually, Peter trusts my common sense more.

"I need you with me," he says, cryptic as ever, and I don't know if he really has a plan or if his mind is playing some sort of trick again. "And Tink."

"Really." Tink arches a brow. "Are you sure you're not confused, King Peter?"

"I'm sure. Take her." He hands Wendy off to Wes and she flattens her mouth and looks like she's about to resist, demand to know more, or worse, demand to go with us—but she sighs and lets Wes lead her away. "And don't fuck her!" Peter calls after them.

Wendy lifts her hand and gives him the finger.

I stifle a snicker and clear my throat.

My God, I'm starting to like this girl.

————

"So what's your idea?" I ask as we trudge among the sparse trees, heading toward the town. "Head Hook off and then?"

"Yeah, Peter Pan, what's your idea?" Tink asks but he glances at me, shadows in his normally bright eyes. He's worried. About Peter? About Hook? About this new Wendy? Who the hell knows?

"We're going to convince him I didn't find Wendy," Peter says, an edge to his voice.

"You mean, the right Wendy?" I mutter.

"Yeah."

"But doesn't that imply..." It's my turn to glance at Tink, looking for some reassurance that I'm not imagining things. "That this is the right Wendy?"

"Yeah," Peter says, more impatiently.

"But didn't we agree... that she's not..."

"No."

Color me confused. Baffled, honestly. Tink looks the way I feel, brows up to his hairline. "Do you mean she is or she isn't the o—"

"See now why you have to keep your hands off her?" Peter

snarls as he stalks off, heading toward the town. "You'll fuck up her magic."

"What the hell are you on about?" Tink strolls after Peter while I stand there, bummed and at the same time buzzing—because dammit, I'm dying to get my dick inside of her but the chance that she may be the one, at long fucking last...

"Try and keep up, Tinkers," Peter says.

"No, man, this won't fly, not like that." Tink's voice is sharp like a blade. "I don't feel any magic in her. Do you? Do you feel, I don't know, magic, or anything that could break the spell, set us free—?"

"She's human," he says.

Tink lets out an incredulous laugh. "Isn't that a *no*?"

Goddammit.

Tink glances back at me, rolls his eyes. "*Crazy*," he mouths at me.

Is he, though? What the hell, is she or isn't she magical? Is she or isn't she the one? It can't be both, and Peter's mind can't be trusted.

Scowling, I follow after them, drawing out my gun, checking the magazine. I have a few bullets left. Not gonna make much of a difference if we have to fight.

We've managed to avoid engaging with Hook's gang for a long time now and last time...

Last time wasn't pretty.

It left us with little ammunition, for starters, and as only Peter can cross over to the real world, we're running low. He hasn't thought to bring any with him this time.

And traveling between worlds makes him sicker. He has a scar that keeps festering, and as it's only half on his physical body, it's impossible to cure.

The Fisher King, Hook calls him—some medieval myth about a king with a wound that can't heal, apparently.

Hook was always one about history and knowledge. He was

the one insisting we should return to the real world back when we didn't give a shit, all too fucking happy to be rid of the real world, to be as far away from it as possible.

Such fucking fools we were.

Still are.

"You still haven't told us your idea, Peter," Tink says, glancing around him, his hand on the pommel of his sword, his magic flaring around him like an aura. "How do you propose to beat Hook?"

"I don't," Peter says. "I can't beat him. I'll just convince him that we have the wrong Wendy once more."

There he goes again, implying she is the right one.

But that's fucking impossible... isn't it?

9

PETER

I *hurt.*

I fucking *hurt.*

Only the real Wendy could make me ache like this.

The thought won't let go, one of the few constants in a world spiraling into madness. She makes me hurt deep in my chest, in my head, unearthing barbed wires and secrets that have remained buried for centuries.

Her presence is digging them up, slowly and excruciatingly, and I don't know how to fucking deal with it.

Especially when I can barely remember how I found her and brought her over. My memory is going. Fickle brain cells. Too damaged by Fae magic and an eternity of fuckery, I'm a king unlike any other.

Half-mad.

Lost.

Confused.

Leader to a bunch of guys as crazy as I am.

King of nothing.

Oh, and kidnapper of girls named Wendy in the hopes that the prophecy will eventually come to pass.

Fat chance.

Except... *Hurt. Pain.* This discomfort inside me when I am around her, making me reach for her, crave her.

Hell.

Am I sure it's her? Fuck, no.

Then again, after centuries of trying, of grabbing girls and bringing them over only to have them lose their minds and take their own lives, I'm not sure about anything. There were girls who lasted over a month with us, until we became attached to them and broke down when they vanished. There were girls that lasted a week.

They all hurt.

From the laws of Neverland.

From us.

I mean, what do you do with a random girl who cries every day to go back home, who fights you and curses you? You lash out. All that pent-up fury and fear, they need an outlet.

Sometimes I wonder if the curse of Neverland is us. If its cruel laws are our laws. If we are the laws.

If we are the new reality of this place.

New. *Huh.* Maybe simply *worse.* Dragging this world down with us. Towns falling to ruin. People vanishing. The woods thinning out. The mermaids—

"Peter, goddammit," Tink says, coming to stand in my way. "Where the fuck are we going? Talk to us."

"Since when do I talk to you?" I growl. "Get out of my face, asshole."

For the flash of an eye, Tink looks stricken. "But—"

"Heading to the center of the island," I say and walk past him, refusing to dwell on that. Maybe I imagined it.

Maybe *I'm* the asshole I accuse him of being.

The two of them grumble as I lead them toward the center, and with good reason, I have to acknowledge. This is the nexus, the fountain of my power, and also the place where I'm at my most vulnerable.

But I'll use my magic to convince Hook that he's wrong, that he misheard, misfelt. That she is not the one.

Am I sure it's her? *Hell, no.*

But for the first time in so long I feel a glimmer of hope.

I don't even know why I think it's her, why I have this feeling that she's the one we've been waiting for when I keep forgetting who she is.

It's just that some things are felt, not known.

Now I just need to stop the other guys from dipping their dick into her and we're golden. Or may one day be golden, if it works out.

And if I still remember my plan and my conviction after this confrontation with Hook is over.

THE ISLAND IS MAGICAL, LIKE THE WHOLE OF NEVERLAND.

What this means is that it's damn inconsistent. It sometimes changes, shifting in small ways, moving a wall here, a tree there. Changing the season. Changing the hour. Changing the monsters' faces.

What that depends on? Time.

The tampering of the Dark Fae with the timespace. Fucking with us all.

Time and Wendy's nightmares.

Another thing that makes me think she's the one, I recall suddenly. She said she remembers this place. When I crossed over with her... I could still recall things, and I was sure then... I was sure it was her, when I was in the real world, watching her, when she was attacked and I caught her—

I almost stumble, caught in this flash of memory, and Colt grabs me to stop me from faceplanting.

"They attacked her," I whisper.

"What, Wendy?" He helps me find my feet. "Who attacked her? Where?"

"In the real world. It was Hook. Hook got to her there. I barely saved her—"

Colt frowns. "Whoa, breathe. Where was that?"

"On the street, close to where she lives. He was going to carry her away, and I stepped between them, and grabbed her—"

"Most probably it was a random thief, man." Colt shakes his head. "Can Hook travel to the real world? That would be a first."

Fuck, yeah, true, and as the details start slipping through my fingers once more. What happened before we crossed makes less and less sense. The venom in my leg burns and I grit my teeth as I reach down to pull my pant leg up.

"We can't go to the center," Tink says and I stop mid-motion. "With the amount of magic there, the venom will spread faster."

"Fuck that," I say, releasing the fabric from my fingers. "I'm fine. We're going, and that's final."

"Is that an order, your Majesty?" he snarks.

"Damn right it is." I yank my arm free of Colt's grip and limp on. "Come on, we haven't got all day."

"You could say that again." Tink tilts his head to the side, pink and copper hair sliding over his face. "Can you hear it?"

Tik-tock.

Hook's watch.

We shouldn't be able to hear it from such a distance, but sometimes the laws of physics are wonky here, allowing the sound of Hook's annoying tik-tocking instrument to reach my ears.

Like right now.

Fuck.

"Run!" I yell and give the example when they just stand there, staring at me. "Run, you fuckers! Run for your lives."

I may forget in a minute what this is all about, but I won't let it fucking stop me from trying to fix this world.

———

THE CENTER IS NOT MARKED BY ANYTHING CONCRETE. IT ALSO shifts, like everything on the fucking island, and currently it's drawing me into the ruins of the town. I haven't been inside its streets in a while, because...

Because I was in the real world.

Right.

Dammit, my mind is starting to slip again.

"Hurry the fuck up," I say and start running full-out toward the heart of the pull, the soles of my boots slapping on cracked concrete, my steps echoing in the quiet. "Come on."

"This is fucked-up," Colt says, running after me. "I hope you haven't forgotten about the natives."

I keep running. "The natives?"

"Yeah, remember?" Tink overtakes me, then slows down again until we're running side by side. "Dammit, you forgot that, too? Where the hell is the center today? Will you be able to find it?"

"Stop talking," I grind out and veer into a side street because obviously I don't fucking remember. My memory is fickle, picking and choosing what to show me. The *tik-tock* follows us and it seems to be growing louder. "Fuck!"

Closer and closer we get, and something flashes out of the corner of my eye—a mismatched red-skinned creature with a wide, fanged mouth, and I throw my hand up and slam my magic into it. It shrieks as it falls apart—and I groan as the pain in my side redoubles.

Almost there.

We skid into an alley with graffiti on the walls and there's... water there? What the fuck? Why is the alley flooded?

"What the fuck?" Colt says, echoing my thoughts, and that's reassuring.

To a point.

"Here," I lie, grabbing my side and gritting my teeth. "We're here. The center is here."

"The water must be because this is her dream," Tink whispers, looking around. "Why the hell is she so afraid of water?"

I know the answer to this, I'm sure I do, but my memory won't give it up. I stumble a few steps and Colt shoves his shoulder under my arm, keeping me upright.

"Come on, Peter," he says. "You can do this."

"Hey, isn't this the place Wes likes so much?" Tink mutters. "That graffiti on the wall..."

"It is."

The center is pulsing nearby, digging claws into my skull. This close to it, I am the island, I am the nightmare. I can feel my face change, my lips retreating, my teeth lengthening, my hair standing up in hardening spikes. My hands turning into claws.

And I feel him. As I turn, pulling Colt around with me, there he stands.

"Hook," I mutter.

"Pan," he returns the greeting, strolling toward us as if nothing is amiss. "What's up?"

Colt pulls out his gun with a curse.

Tink draws his sword from its ancient scabbard, the sound of metal on metal ringing out way too loud.

Hook laughs.

His men stand still behind him, a small group, not an army this time, their steps splashing in the water covering the alley.

He looks... the same as always. Same as the last time I saw

him—same as that time I tried to kill him, my knife in his chest, twisting, his silver pistol on my side, *boom boom boom*, gunshot after gunshot, both of us bleeding and fading...

And yet he's the same, silvery blond hair and gray eyes, dimples in his cheeks. He's wearing a suit, a fucking old-fashioned suit, always.

That's Hook all right. A three-piece suit and a white shirt, hands in his pant pockets, chest thrust out.

Genuine. Warm. Likable.

A fucking bastard.

I feel loopy. I'm running low on fairydust and the cravings are a bitch, but one thing seems to be making sense:

Memory and time.

They're intertwined, aren't they? Sometimes I'm not sure if it's time that acts wonky on the island or if it's the fucking jumble inside my head that makes it seem that way.

Wrong place for an epiphany.

"You don't look so good," Hook says, giving me a critical look. "Has time been wearing you down, Pan?"

"Fuck you," I say. How can he look the same when I'm more scarred inside and out every time we meet?

"Not looking for a fuckbuddy right now, thanks." He eyes Colt and Tink who are still brandishing their weapons. "Tell your friends to relax, will you?"

"You tell them," I mutter.

Hook's brows rise. "You say that so... *deadpan*."

"Hey, that's *my* specialty," Tink complains. "*I* make the puns around here."

"Or is it just pans?" Hook says. "Pans and pots?"

Tink shows his sharp teeth. "That was awful. Painfully bad, Hook."

"Aw, Tinker. That's sweet." Hook takes a step closer. "Don't tell me you missed me?"

Tink growls and takes a fighting stance.

"I'll take that as a *yes*," Hook says. "I'm not even asking Colt, who's so cold inside and out, and as for you... You're just a flash in the pan, aren't you, Peter? Hence the pun with the pans."

"Oh, God, stop it," Tink mutters. "You suck at this wordplay thing. It hurts my brain. Honestly, trust me on this and leave it to the experts."

"I've been outsmarting you for centuries, you bastard, Hook," I say.

"Have you, now? Or have you just been failing to find the one woman you think will save you? And time..." Hook glances at his damn annoying crocodile-skin pocket watch, the source of the maddening *tik-tock* that echoes around the island like a heartbeat. "Time is running out."

"So you say." I straighten, biting back a groan. "So you keep saying. I've got all the time in the world."

"You think you found the right girl this time," Hook says, eyes narrowing to slits.

"I never said that."

"I felt her," he says. "Heard her with you and your boys."

"And you think I'd let them put their paws all over her if she was the one? You think I would touch her if there was a chance she could save us?"

He hesitates, frowns. "You didn't actually fuck her, you or the Lost Boys. I don't believe that for a second."

"Don't you?"

Colt's hold on me tightens. He doesn't know what game I'm playing. That's the idea. If only I can keep my thoughts together a while longer...

"You wouldn't let them even kiss that Wendy back then," Hooks says. "Back when we fought over her. You didn't let *me*."

"Still holding a grudge, I see," I breathe.

"She was the one I wanted," he growls, his calm façade finally fragmenting.

"Yeah. Sorry about that." I shrug, playing it nonchalant,

though the pain of those days, that encounter, still smarts, both in flesh and mind. He really had been into that girl. And I had been into him. Who's keeping count, right? "But business is business."

"You cold bastard," he growls. "You didn't let me help her. And then she was gone."

"They all were," I whisper. Frown. This isn't the game I was planning, this raw pain welling inside of me almost erasing the pain of magic, of the center's pull.

"I thought you'd drag me to the center," he says, "to bespell me, befuddle my thoughts, convince me."

"I never thought that would work," I say and Tink lowers his sword and turns to me, his face a thundercloud.

Yeah, I lied.

I do that. I'm good at that. My whole life is a lie.

And I'm not a good guy. Never said I was.

"Captain," one of Hook's men says and his feet splash in the water. He points and I manage to plaster an expression of curiosity on my face as I turn around to see.

There, caught in a moonbeam, under the graffiti of a crescent moon and a circle of stars.

A disheveled Wendy and a red-faced Wes, kissing.

He has his hands on her face, and she has her arms around his neck, standing on tiptoe to reach him, and it's fucking sweet.

The magic makes me feel sick. The magic that has been tugging on them, pulling them toward us.

They don't call me King for nothing.

"Fuck," Colt hisses. "Didn't he tell you to hide?"

Wes breaks the kiss and his eyes go round. "Oh shit. We were," he hisses right back. "How could I have known you'd come here of all places?"

"Well, hello there," Hook says, his grin sharp. "You must be the new Wendy on the block."

"Wendy Darling," she says, a stubborn tilt to her chin, eyes narrowed and no hint of fear in her blue gaze. "Hook, I presume?"

"You presume right." Hook bows, ever the gentleman, sweeping his hand to the side with a flourish. He has been around as long as I have, unlike the other Lost Boys. No, even longer. "James Hook, at your service. You can call me Jas." Then he turns to me. "Oh... He was kissing her. So it's true. Your plan really didn't pan out, did it?"

"Out of the frying pan and into the fire," I agree and stifle a crazed laugh. "Oh, yeah."

He leans in. "She really isn't the right one."

"Nope."

She's not.

Can you read my thoughts, Jas?

If you are, she's not the one you want.

10

WENDY

My lips burn from Wes' kiss. I don't even know how it happened, how we went from running to kissing.

He's hustled me along into the ruins of the town, seemed to know the way he was taking. Led me down streets overgrown with weeds and buildings crumbling into dust, creepers growing over the walls.

And behind it all was the sound of the sea, a relentless reminder of my nightmares, the waves crashing and crashing, a rhythm, a tide, a heartbeat, a clock ticking down the minutes.

Then we were slogging through an alley and the sea was crashing and filling my senses, and he was pushing me into a building entrance and crushing his mouth against mine.

I mean... he's beautiful. They all are.

And I can't help myself.

Shock after shock has weakened my defenses, my reason. All the pent-up excitement from the bedroom earlier makes me lose all inhibition, needing release, so I kiss him back, rub myself all over his hard body, shutting out the world, forgetting that there is supposed to be danger.

That this Hook guy is after us.

Whoever that is.

And then... Then, voices break through the haze and something *pulls* at us, until Wes walks us backward, back out, into the alley.

There they are, the others—Peter Pan, Colt, Tink, but also a group of unknown men, a silver-haired hunk on the lead.

I mean... God, maybe they should call this place *Hunkland*. Or *Hunk Island*. Is there a single guy who isn't drop-dead gorgeous?

The hunk looks annoyed but then his mouth turns up into a smirk. "You must be the new Wendy on the block."

"Wendy Darling," I say, lifting my chin, refusing to look afraid. "Hook, I presume?"

"You presume right." He bows. "James Hook, at your service. You can call me Jas."

"Jas..." He's dressed in old-fashioned clothes, like Peter, but Hook's are cleaner and better kept. With his silver hair and pale eyes, he looks exotic and also dangerous.

This is the guy the boys are afraid of.

But why?

He says something to Peter about plans not panning out and Peter's mouth twitches as if he wants to grin but won't. Wes is sweating bullets beside me. Obviously kissing me is off limits, for some obscure reason.

Nevertheless, they *have* kissed me. Well, the Twins have. Tink almost did.

Only Peter's mouth has yet to approach mine, a mouth I can't stop looking at.

And now Hook's, too.

Baby Jesus, what's the matter with me? Is it this place? Is it driving me insane, like it has Peter?

"Well, well," Hook says, his gaze locked on me. "Enjoy her while you can, then. I wonder how long this one will last at your hands. A week?"

"What?" My attention is now on Hook. "What are you talking about?"

"Oh, hasn't he told you? Hasn't he warned you?" He tsks. "Bad boy, Pan."

"Shut up," Peter growls.

"Peter used to be such a nice guy," Hook goes on. "Not here, though. Not since the Fae sank their fangs in him and turned him. Since Neverland claimed him. He's a beast inside. A beast he barely controls. He says his memory goes at times. With it goes reason."

"Shut your piehole, Hook," Peter says.

Hook gives a dramatic sigh, his handsome face twisting in a parody of sympathy. "Such a pity. Leaving all the girls behind him like broken dolls to be buried."

"Buried?" Fear bleeds into me, making my breaths short and my head spin. "But—"

"I'll leave you to it," Hook says, turning toward the men behind him. "A pity. This Wendy is actually quite pretty. Goodbye, Wendy Darling. May you rest in peace."

———

"What was he talking about?" I demand. "Rest in peace? What did he mean?"

But the Boys don't seem to be paying me any attention.

"Shut your mouth!" Peter shouts at Hook who doesn't look back as he leaves with his men. "Shut up!"

Hook's words have rattled me. I realize that, despite everything, I had started to relax around my captors.

They haven't actually treated me badly so far, for kidnappers. They haven't hurt me.

In fact, they seemed to be trying to protect me from this Hook guy—but what if I should have gone with him?

Maybe he's the only sane one.

My fears are compounded by the way Peter is hauling me after him, his hand once more like a vise around my wrist. It hurts. I've told him so.

He doesn't appear to give a damn.

"What happened to the other girls you brought here? What happened to them? These other Wendies, where are they?"

No answer.

The others seem to be equally oblivious to my resistance, my questions, my fear. Tink is marching ahead, the pink streaks in his copper hair turned to black once more—probably a bad sign. The Twins are walking far apart, each with a scowl on their handsome faces.

And Peter...

Yeah, Peter is exuding anger, like a fire-breathing dragon.

"Peter," Wes starts—for the fourth time.

Peter says, "Shut up."

"What were the odds of us ending up at the center?" Wes chuckles nervously. "I didn't know—"

"Peter knew you'd be there," Tink says from ahead.

"He did?" Wes turns to Peter, eyes narrowing. "Wait, how could you know, when *I* didn't know we were at the center—"

"That wasn't the center," Tink says. "Was it, Peter?"

"No," Peter says. "It wasn't far, though. By my guess, a few kilometers, give or take."

"But then... why did you go there? Peter." Wes grabs Peter's arm, spins him around. "I'm talking to you."

Peter pulls back his fist and punches Wes square in the face, and I yelp, backtracking, trying to free my wrist from Peter's hold.

No chance of that happening, of course.

"Fuck..." Wes stumbles a few steps back. "What the fuck, man?"

"You're so predictable," Peter growls. "I knew exactly where you would go and what you would try to pull off, despite my warnings."

"Hey, if this is about the kiss..."

"Damn right it is."

"Calm your tits," Tink says, and his voice is cold, too. "You knew they'd be kissing, Peter. Your entire plan hinged on that."

Peter smirks.

"You did?" Wes mutters, wiping at his mouth. His hand comes away streaked with bright blood. His teeth, when he grimaces, are covered in it.

"Yeah, because I expect the worst from people."

"*You*?" Tink has stopped and turned around. "You expect the worst? For fuck's sake, Peter, you think you're some kind of saint or what?"

"Shut up, half-breed."

"Ow," Tink says flatly. "Careful, you'll hurt my feelings."

Okay, this is all too much, what they have said, what they implied, the way they talk to one another.

"What's wrong with all of you?" I shout, try again to pull my arm free of Peter's hold. "You *live* together. Apparently, you have a common goal. Why do you hurt each other? Why—?"

Peter hauls me against him suddenly, crushing me to his side. "I'm their king."

I gape at him. "And you think that makes it okay?"

"You don't get to talk," he snarls.

"Why, because I'll die soon?" My voice is rising and I can't help it. "Isn't that what Hook said?"

"Goddammit." Colt is suddenly there, pulling me away from Peter, and surprisingly, Peter lets go. "Come, Wendy. Let's go home."

"My home isn't here!" I'm shaking and I'm unable to stop. My wrist throbs, my heart aches. "My home is the apartment I share with Charlie, my home is my brothers and my job at the café. Not here!"

"Shush," Colt says, his face tightening. "You're not going back there, so stop talking about it. Easier that way. And stop thinking of running away. There's no way back from Neverland, do you hear me?"

Numb, I let him lead me away.

———

THE FOOD THE TWINS COOKED EARLIER HAS TURNED COLD AND soggy.

Despite his protests earlier about not cooking, however, Tink takes over and warms the food up in a pot, then dishes it out on chipped plates he places around the table, along with tarnished silverware and mugs for the water.

So domestic and quiet after our flight and fright, after the arguments and shoving around.

So homey and so fake.

I'm still shaking. I still don't know what the hell I'm doing here, except I'm apparently to be sacrificed to the altar of mad gods and mad men.

Peter doesn't join us. He lies down on the sofa, turns his back on us, and seems to go straight to sleep.

I can't miss the way the boys keep casting worried glances his way, though. And I shouldn't care. Shouldn't be worried.

I'm not, all right? I'm worried about myself, that's all. And I distract myself with the food, because dwelling on all that has happened today is bound to eat away at the last of my sanity. I chew the meat that has begun to harden to avoid a different kind of rumination.

Stop thinking, I tell myself. *Just eat and rest. Panicking all over again won't help now.*

God, I wish Charlie were here with me.

Then again, no, I wouldn't want her to be in such danger. Better that I'm on my own with these psychos.

Said psychos are making short work of the food, tearing into the meat, chucking the veggies into their mouths as if their gullets are black holes, swallowing everything.

They don't seem overly concerned about my impending death or Hook's forces, Peter's madness or any of this crazy mess.

"So tell us," Tink asks, when he finally pushes his empty plate away, "why don't you like the sea? Most people do."

"I'm not most people," I mumble, shoving my food around my plate with my fork. "I'm just me."

He leans forward. "What happened to you, Wendy?"

... hands pulling me down into the dark and the cold... seagrass waving around me, the ribbons of my dress floating around me, my hair fanning around my face like a yellow anemone, poison seeping into me as I try and fail to draw breath...

"I don't want to talk about it," I whisper.

"Oh, come on, Wendy," Tink says. "Spill."

"It's none of your business!"

He harrumphs. "You're as prickly as Peter."

"Don't compare me to him," I hiss. "He's a psycho."

"He changed," Tink says, a small frown on his face. "Both he and Hook changed. Time has worn their edges down, like the sea eats at the rocks."

"Now you'll be telling me he used to be a nice guy, like Hook said?" I almost shout.

"I wouldn't say that. Wouldn't go that far." Tink huffs. "Some dark impulses run deep, you know."

I shiver.

"But he never confused his desires with his duties before," Tink goes on, softly. "He didn't confuse reality with fantasy."

"What...?" I swallow hard, stirring the veggies in my plate some more. "What about the other girls Hook mentioned? Tink, you told me... You said the other Wendies went mad and jumped off the cliffs. But Hook made it sound like... the girls went mad because of you. All of you. Or maybe just Peter."

They exchange uncomfortable glances.

"Is he going to kill me?" I whisper into the growing silence.

"What? No. He's not a killer." Colt puts his fork down. "I mean, not on purpose."

Jesus on a stick. "Meaning what?"

"He just... loses control sometimes." Colt shrugs. "During sex."

"Loses control? Only during sex?" Got to get those details clear, right?

Colt sighs. "He's a... a dominant. Who can't always control his urges. And he likes to cause pain."

"So he's a sadist."

"Yeah." Another shrug, "Girls seem to find it... traumatic."

"Christ. And you?"

"You're asking if I'm a sadist?" Colt turns his gaze away. "I guess all of us here are into pain. And violence. The thing with this place is that... it breaks down your control, you see. We fuck violently. And some girls can't take it. Physically. Or mentally."

"We fuck violently." What the hell? He says it like it's something normal, something everyone has to deal with. Losing control with a girl.

And why do I throb down below when I should be screaming and running for the door, no matter the consequences?

PART II

"Never is an awfully long time."
— J.M. Barrie, Peter Pan

11

WENDY

"Fuck violently, huh?" I stab at my greens, clear my throat. My face is starting to burn. "But Peter says you're not supposed to even kiss me."

"Tough." Wes snickers. "And too late."

My mouth tries to smile but I don't let it. "Why not, then?"

"If you guys hadn't showed up," Wes goes on, nodding at Colt and Tink, "I'd have taken you against the wall, girl." He leans back, rubs his crotch. "You were ready for it."

I was, truth be told, and the heat rises to my face. "Tell me why Peter doesn't want you kissing and touching me. You can't keep changing the topic with sex."

Wes smirks. "Why not? Seems to work just fine."

"*Why not*? *Jesus*. Tell me what this is about, why I am here!" I throw my hands in the air. "Find a way for Hook not to hear us and just tell me."

"Oh, Hook knows you're here now. It's moot. Might as well tell you."

"Then what are you waiting for?"

He turns to the others. "Were the Wendies always so impatient and annoying?"

"I'm not *a* Wendy! I'm Wendy Darling. An actual person! Start treating me like one."

"And demanding," Wes says thoughtfully. "So very demanding. I wonder how you are in the sack."

"Wouldn't you like to know?" I lean forward, stare him down. "Huh?"

He laughs. "Well, Peter said you're not the one, so... why the hell not, right guys? We can tell you. And we can fuck you, too."

"That was a trick," Tink says softly. "To convince Hook. She's the one."

"She is? But I did kiss her," Wes says.

"So did I," Colt says. "If she was the one, wouldn't it be too late?"

"You, jackasses." Tink smirks. "You're turning as forgetful as Peter now? Kissing won't change her. *Fucking* her will."

"But then why didn't he let us kiss—?"

"Because kissing leads to fucking. Kissing leads to loss of control. You—"

"Change me?" I interrupt. "Change me how? What do you think I can do?"

"Save us," Colt says, his dark gaze earnest and clear. "Save this world. Turn off the nightmare. Return it to the dream it used to be. It—"

"Fuck, shut up, Colt!" Tink slams his hands on the table and gets up. "We've said too much."

"She's not the one, Tink." Wes shakes his head. "You know Peter. His mind's a mess."

"He's right, you know," a voice says from the kitchen doorway, and I flinch. "I'm a fucking mess."

"Come eat, Peter," Tink says, his voice hard. "And stop—"

"But," Peter says, "she's not the one."

"Oh, for fuck's sake!" Tink's eyes blaze. "When will you stop lying? Pick a story and run with it, will you? She is the one. She's not. Let's go to the center. Oh, no, let's go to town and set it up so that Hook sees Wendy with Wes. Lie to Hook. Lie to us again. Change the story for the thousandth time, then—"

"You exaggerate," Peter mutters, limping inside and coming to stand behind a chair.

"Do I?" Tink snaps, leaning back in his chair, folding his arms over his chest. "I don't even know what is real anymore."

"Nothing here is real," Peter says, his voice also turning to steel.

"Is that so? Then why are we still trying?" Tink mutters. "I don't know if all you do and say is an act or if your memory is really going and…"

Peter says, "Aw, are you worried for me, Tink?"

Tink freezes, eyes wide.

Then he shrugs his broad shoulders, a defiant look in his eyes, rapidly solidifying into anger. "Fuck you." He gets up, gives Peter the finger and leaves the room.

There's a beat of heavy silence.

"Dammit, man," Colt breathes, pushing his plate away. "Stop fucking with our heads. Is she or isn't she the one?"

"Only one way to know," Peter says, his gaze finally landing on me, cold and hot at once. "Isn't there?"

"Are you asking me?" I grumble. "For real?"

"She already changed the island," Wes says. "Through her nightmares."

"Though not for the better," Colt says with a shrug.

"Question is…" Peter is still gazing at me. "Can she change it more? Can she make it better? Can you, Wendy?"

"Change the island?" I whisper.

"Change Neverland."

I hold his gaze. "How can I do that?"

"That is the question, isn't it? I don't know."

"Then what am I supposed to do?" I ask.

"How about you try it in your sleep," Peter says. "Dream of better things."

"Easy for you to say."

"Is it?" His voice drops, low and delicious and lethal. "If my dreams had shaped this place, it would look like the ninth circle of hell."

I shake my head. "That's not helping."

"Peter gets bad dreams," Wes says slowly. "Screaming bad. We all sleep badly, but Peter's are the worst."

"What is it to me?" I whisper, fighting the sympathy, knowing it's a bad idea. "You took me from my home, brought me here to use my dreams?"

"That's right."

Anger rises in a hot, red tide. "How about no? How about asking me first before you use anything of mine?"

"This isn't up to us, girl. Or to you." His eyes are flat and hard, "The magic. Your connection to us."

"Just like that, huh? Not up to you? You're the ones who brought me here!"

"Enough," Peter says, his voice harsh. "Bed time." He nods at the Twins. "Take her. Time to use her."

————

Use me?

I yell at them to stop, I fight them. It's not the thought of going to bed that has me panicking, I'm bone-weary—but after all the things they said... I don't know what they're planning to do with me.

"Don't touch me!" I try to bite Colt's hand as he lifts me in his arms and strides out of the kitchen. I slap his face. "Let me down!"

He says nothing.

I twist and shove at his arms. "What will you do to me? Use me how?"

No answer.

Pushing me down on the bed, they tie my hands over my head, to the bars of the iron headboard, as I squirm and kick. Tink is nowhere to be seen. Peter appears at the door of the bedroom as Wes goes around the bed to test the knots.

"Let me go!" I yell. "Untie me!"

"We're just making sure you won't run away," Wes says.

"Run away, how? I'm locked in here! What do you want with me?"

"You asked how we plan on using you." He bares his teeth in a grin. "We want you to dream. Dream of something good, will ya?"

"Good?" I kick right and left but they act like they don't feel it. "Good how?"

"God above, girl. Haven't you ever had good dreams? Dreams where you feel safe and warm and comfortable, where you feel like you belong and everything will be okay?"

"No," I say sullenly. "Have you?"

He gives a harsh bark of a laugh. "Just go to sleep."

"You just like tying me up!" I yell at the Twins as they walk out of the room. "Don't you? It makes you hard when I'm scared. All of you. It turns you on."

Peter is the last one remaining at the door. I open my mouth to yell some more, to curse him, insult him with the best swearwords I know, when he reaches down and grabs his cock through his pants, giving it a squeeze. His eyes darken.

Well, Christ. I was right. He's hard. Very hard.

An image hits me. What if they used me like this? Not my dreams, but my body. Tied up on the bed, what if they pulled down my panties and just... pleasured me? Or took their own pleasure?

Oh God...

The throb between my legs returns, insistent, almost painful, and I swallow a moan. Mortified, my cheeks on fire, I roll my head on the pillow to face away and close my eyes.

Enough, I tell myself. *Stop with these crazy thoughts. Just sleep.*

———

IN MY DREAM, I'M DROWNING.

The ruined town has sunk under the water, graffiti-covered walls surrounding me as I sink. Fish swim by, silver flashes. Bubbles wobble.

My hair rises at my sides like tentacles, wrapping around me, choking me.

I start struggling as my lungs constrict. *No air.* I have to breathe. Can't. Suffocating. Drowning. Dying.

Please...

Strong hands grab me, stopping my descent. Pulling me up.

"There, there," a low male voice says, a familiar voice. A light touch on my face, then a spicy scent envelops me. "Just dream, sweetheart. No nightmares."

The hands pull me out of the water and my chest expands, pulling in sweet oxygen. I cling to the man as he carries me out.

And then the scene changes unexpectedly—in the way dreams do—and I'm on the floor, a heavy body pressing down on mine and I like it.

I like it way too much. Need it. Crave it.

I strain, unable to use my hands to touch. The throbbing between my legs is maddening. I ache. I want... I need...

"Wendy..."

The whisper is the only warning I get before the world shifts—the weight on my body vanishes, and my skirt is pushed up, exposing my panties. I blink, the light too sharp, blinding—but a man with a bright halo like a saint is kneeling between my legs on the bed.

I'm on a bed.

Not a street.

Yet I can still hear the sea, the crashing waves in the

distance, and the hot guy sitting on the bed winks at me before he puts his hands on said panties and yanks.

Just like in my fantasy, I think dimly, as he drags the panties down my legs, the lace whispering against my skin.

"Wes," I breathe as he works the panties off my legs and tosses them to the side.

Another guy climbs onto the bed and I gasp before I recognize Colt, his dark hair loose on his shoulders, his gaze smoldering.

Am I awake?

Wes lifts one of my feet and pulls off my boot and stocking, letting both fall off the side of the bed, while Colt does the same with the other foot.

Wes bends and trails his lips over my inner thigh. Then I flinch when something cold trails after the warmth of his mouth over my knee and then my thigh.

"Wes?" I whisper.

"Sh..."

I gulp. "I thought... Peter said..."

"Yeah, well, he said no fucking, but nobody said anything about using my hands. Or my mouth. Or my toys."

"Toys?"

And he lifts his gun. "Boom," he says and grins.

12

WENDY

At first, I think he's kidding.

His gun? I mean, I can't even fathom what he means to do with it, but then...

Then he shoves the gun into me.

Into my pussy.

The barrel of the frigging gun—slowly, inexorably, making me gasp and squirm. It's like a dildo, but so cold and hard. Unforgiving.

"What... what are you doing?" I pant. "Wes?"

"I think it's obvious."

"Wait, Wes—"

"I'm fucking you with my favorite gun." His grin is crooked and his golden eyes are heavy-lidded. "My gun is an extension of my dick."

"... are you serious?" I manage, squirming as he gives the gun one last little push.

"As a heart attack." He draws back and gets off the bed, leaving his gun lodged inside me, the handle sticking out between my legs.

Where is he going?

"Wes!" I shout. "No! Come back."

Colt distracts me, though, bending over me and trailing his gun down my jaw. "So pretty..."

"Colt!" Fear makes it hard to breathe. "Colt, take that gun out of me. Please, take it out..."

"Mm... I like seeing it there. Time to make room for mine, too."

"Yours?" He strokes the barrel of his gun over my chin, taps it on my lips. I turn my head to the side. "No. I can't."

"Would you rather I left now?"

"No! Please. You can't leave me like this!" Tears leak from the corners of my eyes. "You... assholes. Please..."

"You talk too much. Peter will hear us. So..." Colt pushes the barrel of his gun into my mouth. "Make love to it, baby."

I gag.

And I throb.

And I don't know what is going on with my body because it's never felt so hot and tight, clenched so tightly.

I've never been on the cusp of a mind-shattering orgasm by being tied up and fucked with guns—like, hell no. I never had fantasies like that. I mean I did fantasize about a guy shoving me up against furniture, grabbing me roughly, stuff like that, but this?

Never even knew that gunplay was a thing. A thing that got me aroused.

Or maybe it's their faces, gazes gone dark and hazy, mouths slightly parted, muscular chests rising and falling as if they've been running, their cocks tenting their pants like never before.

I'm doing this to them. Handling me like this makes them so hard their cocks look just about ready to bust the seams.

But they don't do anything about it. They don't free their cocks, touch them, they don't linger. With one last look at me, stuffed with their guns on both ends, they walk out of the room, leaving me to scream soundlessly at them.

Oh God... What now?

———

I'm choking. I can't breathe. It's as if I'm back underwater. The room is dimly lit, with glow stars stuck on the ceiling, a bit like my room when I was growing up.

I'm falling, and I'm panicking, and every shift of my body on the bed, every shallow breath, seems to stoke the fire in my belly.

This is insane.

More tears leak from my eyes. They can't leave me like this, can they? It's... dangerous. Scary. Humiliating. They brought me here for a reason, an obscure reason, true, but still...

Peter seemed convinced I'm the one—whatever that means. He wouldn't let me suffocate. He wouldn't let them harm me.

I cling to that belief as time grinds by, the soughing of the waves marking it like a metronome, like the island is a giant clock and the sea its pendulum.

God.

Can't.

Every movement jostles the gun inside me, makes me gag on the other gun in my mouth, and I don't know how long I will last—

"Wendy?" Tink steps inside the room a minute or maybe a year later, impossible to tell, and stops. "What in the ever-loving fuck?"

I yell at him, muffled by the gun. Its barrel is too thick, holding my jaw wide open, making it impossible to spit it out.

Then he starts laughing. "Oh, my fucking god. Those fucking Twins. I leave the house for five minutes and I come back to this?"

"Tink," I try to say and choke on the gun.

"Of course, they found a loophole," he mutters to himself.

"Hands, mouth, toys... They could have used some of our toys. Dildos. Vibrators. Nipple clamps... but no, they had to go for their own favorites."

I choke again, and now I can't breathe at all.

Finally, Tink takes pity on me. He comes around the bed and pulls the gun out of my mouth.

I gasp for breath, saliva running down my chin. "Tink! Help me!"

"I just did," he says, lifting the gun, then tossing it on the bed. "You're welcome."

I pull on the ropes tied around my wrists. "The other one! Please."

"Hm... I don't know." He strokes his chin. "It looks good in you."

"You're all psychos!" I yell at him, pulling harder on the ties around my wrists. "Take it out. Tink! Please!"

"Is it uncomfortable?" he asks.

"Yes!"

"Are you sure?"

"Yeah!"

"I think I'll leave it there," he says.

"What? Why?"

He's still stroking his chin. "I like it."

"But I don't! Untie me!"

"Oh, Wendy, Wendy..." Tink shakes his head. "Why do you still think we're *nice*? We are the ones who kidnapped you. Did you forget?" He leans over me, teeth bared. "Then again, this place makes everyone forget. Some more than others."

"What's happening to all of you...?"

"You see what you want to see," Tink continues, his eyes darkening, his wings springing out of his back. "Such a human thing."

"You're half *human*, too!"

"Yeah, that sucks."

"Tink... Peter said I'm the right one."

"Yeah, and? He said lots of things. Whether you're the right girl or not, we can't get attached to you. So we have to punish you."

"You're making no sense!" The barrel of the gun, lodged so deep inside me, is jostled when I twist on the bed, making me gasp.

"So you say. The gun stays." And yet Tink doesn't walk away. Instead, he approaches the bed, his gaze heated, eyes locked between my spread legs. His wings have vanished again, but the darkness in his eyes remains.

"You're not evil," I whisper.

"Aren't we?" His voice is a whisper. "You're aroused by us, you lust after us, you like us touching you, kissing you. But we never did any of that for you. Only for ourselves. For our own pleasure. Our own excitement."

"Please..."

"So tell me, little human girl... Are you so aroused you want to weep? Ready to combust with need? Your blood burning in your veins, between your legs? Is it your wish to be allowed to come?"

Hot tears slip from the corners of my eyes, just as the confession slips from my lips. "Yes."

"I didn't hear you." His voice is a low rasp. "Repeat it for me."

"Yes! I said yes."

He grins. "Then beg for it. Beg if you want my help. Go on. Let me hear it loud and clear."

I draw a shaky breath, and oh God, I'm going to do it, I'm going to beg... when a shadow falls over us.

A shadow long and jagged, dark and ominous, crawling over the floor, climbing the bed.

The King is here.

"What the fuck are you doing?" Peter snarls, lips pulled

back, baring his teeth, hands clenched into tight fists. His eyes burn.

"Well, hello to you too," Tink mutters, his grin falling. "What does it look like I'm doing?"

"Only *I* can hurt her!" Peter growls.

"Well, she's not hurt," Tink says. "And fuck you."

"Get out!"

"Oh, I'm going." Tink casts me a thoughtful look. "Sorry, girl. He's the King. Maybe now you'll decide you like the barrel of a gun better than the knife."

What does he mean?

"Out!" Peter grabs Tink and all but throws him out of the room, slamming the door shut behind him.

"Oh God..." I squirm, tug harder on the ties. "Don't... Just..."

Peter comes around the bed on the other side, still snarling, his broad-shouldered form looming over me.

Right now, he doesn't look quite human, and his fury shakes me, shakes the bed, the house.

The entire island.

"How fucking dare they," he barks. "Those motherfuckers."

Yep, he's furious, and I'm trembling, so frigging deathly scared and also so aroused I can't bear it.

Peter's nearness is like a cold wind, sending waves to stroke my skin, raising goosebumps. My breasts ache, my nipples are diamond-hard, and I'm wound up inside, so close to coming...

He bends over me, his eyes gone black like the pits of hell, his bared canines sharp. No, he doesn't look entirely human right now.

"You're mine," he snarls. "Fucking mine." He growls, and the shadow behind him seems to grow larger and move along the walls on its own, a hulking shape of a beast. I stare at it, uncomprehending.

Then he grabs the handle of the gun between my legs. Pulls it out an inch, shoves it back inside.

Again.

And I shatter. I come apart with a cry, shaking on the bed as wave after wave of pleasure crashes into me, rushes through my body, as my pussy clenches hard, again and again.

Peter swears, though I can't make out the words, lost in the storm raging inside my body. The barrel is still inside me and I'm still coming, weeping and wailing with my release.

It takes me some time to realize he never even once asked if I slept, if I dreamed, if I even tried to do his bidding.

He leans over me, lips peeled back, and I finally realize what has just happened:

Peter has lost control.

13

PETER

I'm grinning like a skull, gazing down at Wendy as she wheezes, still caught in her orgasm, her legs trembling, her chest heaving. The gun is still inside her pussy that's dripping juices all over the covers.

I can fucking smell her cream. Smell the sweetness of it. The flush on her neck and cheeks is bright red, and I imagine it spreading down, over her tits. I can imagine the swell of them, the hard nipples. I lick my lips and I can almost taste her skin, salt and sugar and roses and pretty girl.

It's driving me wild, and that means... mad.

Madder.

I can feel my mind slipping, my shadow detaching, my memory fading. As I stand there, I don't know who I am and who she is, only that she smells good.

Too damn good.

Delicious. Buttery. Soft. Honeyed. Everything I don't have in my life, everything I'm starving for. A full dessert buffet.

And I crave her sugar.

Still vibrating with dark energy, I bend my head, sniff at her skin where her neck meets her shoulder. I lick at it.

Being here with her is bad.

Dangerous.

Fucking lethal.

I knew it from the first moment I saw her, I think, I knew she'd be my fucking undoing, and frown as the memory slips out of my fingers again.

I stalk around the bed once more, taking in the whole of her, so wanton, limbs loose, legs spread, the gun sticking out of her pussy looking so... wrong and yet right, so depraved and sexy.

Her hands are still tied over her head and her sweater and shirt have ridden up a little, too, showing me the black lace of her bra. Her blond hair spills around her head like a sunburst.

Her cheeks are red, her lids heavy, her mouth bee-stung.

She's beautiful.

Hot.

I want her. Have wanted her for a long time. Yeah, I fucking want her and I take what I want. I want...

"Hell." I shake my head to clear it but it only ratchets up the tension, the headache spiking behind my eyes. "Goddammit."

With another curse, I make a quick job of untying her wrists and she moans as her hands fall limply on the pillow by her head.

I stare down at her. Why shouldn't I have her? Why the hell not? I can't... fucking remember. Who is she? What's her name?

Does it matter?

"Peter," she rasps.

"Don't say my name," I growl. *Dangerous,* I think again. I'm not letting her get under my skin, gripping me, changing me. I grab her shoulders, slam her to the bed. "Don't."

She moans.

I stare at her. Am I the crazy one, or is she? "Aren't you scared?"

Now she whimpers.

"You should be." I slam her back to the mattress.

Instead of yelling at me, she lets out a breath, her lashes lowering and her breathing changing—and I can smell her arousal flare.

Sugar and roses.

Fuck.

It messes with my head, grabs me by the balls, by the cock, and won't let go. A pretty, aroused girl in my bed, at my mercy, ready for the taking, and more than that...

More than the power trip...

What? What, Peter? What the fuck are you forgetting now?

It doesn't fucking matter.

Grabbing the handle of the gun, I yank it out of her, wrenching another whimper from her throat, and throw it aside.

Then I lie over her, press her down with my entire body, crushing her smaller, curvy one into the lumpy mattress, my breathing shallow, my dick rock hard. I press my knee between her legs and she moans, eyes fluttering closed.

I press my hand to her neck, cutting off her air and she arches up, rubbing against me.

She likes it.

God fuck.

Red descends over my vision. My shadow spreads, pulls, making my spine bow. It gathers itself from my body, my flesh and bones, from under my skin and inside my veins, rising.

And then it shoves claws into me, entering me instead of wandering, taking over me.

It's an alien thing and yet it's mine, it's me but it has been apart from me for so long—barely attached to me like a graft on a tree that hasn't quite caught—that it has a form and life of its own.

It's everything that's dark in me, and that's a fucking lot. Dark desires, dark thoughts, dark dreams, dark wishes. The animalistic part of me, the one with fangs and claws, the one that bites and scratches and fucks like a beast.

I am it, and it is me. We're one right now, and fleetingly I think that I'm fucking thankful we're usually apart, even if it hurts like a bitch, because my shadow is a motherfucker.

It pushes into me, through me, taking me over—and I grab her blouse, tear it off her, shredding it into strips. Her tits are full and round, encased in fine black lace, her nipples pink and hard.

So easy to tear the lace off her, my nails leaving red lines on her pale skin, on the mounds of her tits. She arches up when I slide my hands over her curves.

I take her nipples between my fingers and twist.

She cries out, gripping my forearms, her own nails digging into my shirt, into my muscles underneath the fabric, and another dark rush goes through me, another red tide rising over my eyes.

My shadow roars.

I cup her neck again, pressing my thumb against her windpipe, cutting off her air, and think of my knives. Of drawing a different kind of red line on her skin, of watching the blood well up.

Fuck, I'm so hard right now.

She's gasping for breath and I let up just a little, letting air trickle into her lungs. She's making these little kittenish noises of need and pleasure, and how the fuck is she aroused by my roughness when other girls run away screaming?

Damn.

It's feeding the beast inside of me, feeding my arousal until my balls are like millstones and my dick a leaden club trying to drill a hole through my pants.

With a curse, I sit back as she coughs and gasps, tears spilling from the corners of her eyes, and unbuckle my belt, undo the button and yank my zipper down, almost ripping my pants in two.

Then I'm on her again, shoving my dick into her wet pussy without any fucking preamble. Ready or not...

But she's ready, alright. Fucked into an orgasm with a gun. Dripping and hot, loosened enough for my dick to wedge itself inside.

It's a tight fit, of course. It always is. And as her gasps turn into hiccuping breaths and she tries to shove me off her, fear making a return, so my pleasure grows.

Pressing her back down, I grab one of her legs and lift it. She curls it around my thigh instinctively and I slide in deeper, a groan making its way past my lips.

So damn good. So damn snug. So fucking tight.

Hot like hell.

And she looks even hotter, her cheeks flushed, eyes wide, her hands that were trying to shove me away now clawing at my arms.

I grunt as I thrust harder, wedging my dick just a little deeper. It won't fit completely, it never does, and—

Her other leg lifts, curls around my other thigh, and she opens up a tiny bit more, just enough—

Oh fucking dammit.

Her lashes lower, her head falls back and her mouth drops open on a long moan as I somehow push inside of her all the way.

It's never happened before, in all my long fucking years. Never had a girl to take me in completely.

Her pussy grips me so tightly I can't fucking breathe, my dick swelling more, twitching. My shadow jerks and twists. The dark spills inside me like ink, spreading, making my spine bow and my muscles clench, my stomach cramping from the force of it.

Oh. Fuck. Me.

Fuck.

Crashing down on my elbows on the mattress, I cage her head with my arms as I start fucking her, my hips rocking with a will of their own, my body chasing its release with a single-mindedness that won't allow me any room to think.

I'm about to come and at this point, I don't give a shit if she gets any pleasure from it or not. She's a convenient hole, that's it. A convenient body to use for my own damn needs, just another nameless girl, a random victim.

And yet something is different, something draws me to her pretty face, her blue eyes. I recall the feel of her delicate wrist in my grip, her low voice and I...

Her pussy pulses around my cock, and a sound escapes me —half surprise and half pain at the punch of pleasure in the gonads. My goddamn ass clenches, my balls detonate, and fuck, since when did I get so out of control?

My head drops forward and shudders shake my frame as I shoot my load. The dark explodes inside of me, dark stars and supernovas, my soul sucked into black holes, vanishing into nothingness.

Empty, aching where my shadow pulls, aching fucking *everywhere*, I slump on top of her. I frown down at her flushed face.

"Don't I know you?" I breathe, smoothing my thumb over her velvety lips, her silky cheekbone. Her hair is silky, too, shorter strands tickling my palm when I brush them off her forehead.

There's that faint scent of roses once more.

She's like the sleeping beauty in the woods, that briar rose, and I'm the hunter who woke her up and carried her away.

Unless I'm the darkness that bound her there in the first place.

The shadow drains out of me, slides away, the tether

between us stretching. It's always near, always a part of me, but my head is a little clearer now.

And she muddles my thoughts again when she puts her hands on my face and tugs me down.

"What are you doing?" I'm staring into her blue eyes. We're nose to nose, both of us breathing hard.

She lifts her head, presses her lips to my mouth. "Kissing you?"

"Oh fuck no." I start to push up, feeling her fingertips trail down my face as I lift myself off her. "I don't kiss. Never kissed anyone."

Why do I still feel her touch on my jaw, on my cheeks? Why do I already miss it as I get off the bed? What's this weird tug inside my chest?

I fight the feeling, throttle it.

Her voice is a breath. "Peter—"

No.

I tuck my cock in, zip up my pants. My shadow rolls against the walls, and I hide a wince. *Hell.* This was a goddamn mistake. I don't do this face to face. I never fuck a girl face to face. Never let our lips touch.

I don't let them touch me, kiss me, speak my name so softly.

I don't let them get to me, get under my skin.

So how is she doing it?

The door opens and Tink stands in the opening. "Peter, the island is changing and..." His eyes widen, then narrow. A glare settles over his features. "Peter, goddammit!"

"What do you want?" I growl.

"What I *want*?" Tink shakes his fist at me. "You, asshole. You said... you said she's the one and that we're not supposed to fuck her."

"I said that? She is?" I turn to look at the girl on the bed who is slowly sitting up, debauched and sexy with her tits bare, her skirt rucked up and her pussy glistening with her release and mine. Tears shine on her cheeks.

"Fuck, Peter," Tink breathes.

Fuck indeed.

"This was a mistake," I say slowly.

But... she was asleep. She was dreaming... Dreaming of me. Dreaming of this.

It was her dreams. They drew me to her. It looks like they drew all of us, but I'd bet my right nut that the others didn't experience her nightmares.

I did. I always do. My bad dreams aren't all mine.

But on their heels came this image of me between her legs, holding her down, pounding into her, and it woke me up with a start. Brought me to her.

How can this be a mistake?

"Tink, you said the island changed?" I drag a hand through my hair and sigh, still gazing at her. "Show me."

"What about Wendy?" he breathes.

"Yes," the girl says, not bothering to wipe the tears off her face, toying with the little thimble pendant hanging around her neck—Wendy, that's her name, right, then again it always is—"what about me?"

"I don't give a shit," I mutter, feeling again that inexplicable tug in my chest and ignoring it as best I can. "Sleep. It's what all hapless humans do."

14

WENDY

"You can sleep, Peter. I've seen it," I mutter and wipe at the tears still leaking from my eyes. "And Tink said you dream, too. So don't give me that 'you humans' crap."

He doesn't reply.

Figures.

God, I need to stop crying.

What the hell, right? How can these boys take me from the highest high to rock bottom in the blink of an eye, making me feel so good, then humiliating me, over and over? They are the most confusing people I've ever met.

The issue is why I like them at all.

I *don't*, I decide. Lust is one thing, but liking them... No. Hell, no. My body is confused. They act... erratically. They go from kind and nice to violent and weird in seconds.

And... and it's exciting. Arousing. This game of fear and pleasure.

God. I put my hands over my face, take a few deep breaths. What's wrong with me?

Seriously, what's wrong with me?

Half-naked on this strange bed, my sweater and shirt

shredded, my bra torn, my panties... gone somewhere, leaking cum between my legs.

Coming so hard from their manipulation of my body like never before, torn between terror and passion all the time.

A rollercoaster of sensations and emotions that's left me so drained I could just lie back down and go to sleep.

If only I didn't feel so guilty for enjoying it.

For liking it.

For craving it.

Is it my past? Does it have to do with my father and the games he played with me? Is it a scar inside of me that makes me this way? How bad of a timing is it that I had to fully uncover this long-suspected side of me on this cursed island, with these cursed boys?

I mean, I knew that nice and gentle wasn't doing it for me, but this?

This is sick.

And I loved every frigging minute of it.

Yes, looking back... even the fear. Especially the fear. It made everything sharp and bright, heightened every sensation, honed every slice of pleasure.

I'm sick. I'm strange.

This is so wrong.

So why does it feel right? Why do I crave it so much?

Dressed only in my short skirt and the shreds of my sweater, shirt and bra, I get off the bed, I go to the door and try it. It swings open.

I don't see anyone outside.

This is wrong and I need to get away.

Covering my boobs with my hands, I walk into the living room. I need clothes. I can't wander around like this. Where do they keep their clothes? I haven't seen a single closet in the entire house.

The shutters on the windows are wooden, painted blue, and through the slats, I see green foliage.

Which is odd. Wasn't the house underground?

It's quiet. Too quiet. Have they left me here alone? Is it possible, after all the talk about keeping an eye on me, stopping me from running but also protecting me?

Or is it safe now that they apparently convinced Hook—*Jas* —that I'm not the one they've been looking for?

But then why was Tink so upset? And Peter... why did he sound like he was regretting fucking me?

"This was a mistake."

Way to crush a girl's heart.

I shiver as I walk through the empty rooms. My heart is safe. Has to be. Lust and horniness are one thing, but this isn't love.

Don't think for one second that it could be anything more.

Where is the kitchen? It was right here. And the living room... I stop in front of the sofa. Which used to be brown. I am pretty sure of it.

Now it's blue, like the window shutters. In fact... Now that I'm thinking about it, I don't recall shutters when we arrived here.

Or windows.

Which makes perfect sense in an underground bunker.

What is going on?

"The island is changing," Tink had said.

What sort of changes are we talking about here?

On the sofa, I find a wrinkled, stained white T-shirt, and pulling off my shredded clothes, leaving on only my short skirt, I pull the T-shirt on. I expect it to stink but in fact it smells of male musk and soap.

For the first time I examine my ruined garments and the red scratches on my skin, and *whoa*. What did this? What I mean is... it doesn't look like the work of human hands, more like... scissors. Or blades.

Or claws.

What the hell? Peter did this. His hands were bare.

Bare and... *Bare hands. Without any ink.* How is this possible?

His ink vanished as his shadow rose, a monster, sliding along the walls—and then it had sort of slammed into him. Or so it had seemed at the time.

Becoming a part of him again.

Not sure of what I saw, really. I had been a little preoccupied with the way he'd been touching me, his hand on my neck, cutting off my air supply, on my nipples, hurting them, then his cock inside of me, so big as he'd rammed it in...

And then the pleasure that went on and on, unlike anything I'd ever experienced before. Anything I'd ever imagined. My sexual fantasies were always far and in between and this... it beat them all.

My boobs covered up, feeling a little better, I walk over to the house door and open it. Look outside.

Right. Of course they didn't leave me alone. Kidnappers aren't that stupid, even if they act so damn weird sometimes.

The Twins are standing outside, mirror images of each other, arms folded over broad chests, matching scowls on their handsome faces. Colt has pulled his dark hair back in a man-bun once more, though a few loose strands soften the hard line of his jaw, whereas Wes's blond hair falls in his face.

Twins and yet... one seems to be the other's shadow, and I don't know if the shadow is prettier than the real thing.

It's impossible to choose.

"You," I snap.

Their gazes swing around to me, flat and unsurprised.

"The princess is up," Wes says.

"Princess? *Really?* Is this how you'd treat one?" I demand, putting my hands on my hips. "Fucking her with your guns?"

Their scowls turn to frowns, as if they're giving my question some actual thought, as if they find it intriguing and unexpected.

"Why not?" Colt eventually asks and sounds actually curious.

"*Why not?*" I echo, blinking at him. "Oh, my God. Are you seriously asking me this?"

"Didn't you enjoy it?" Wes asks.

"I..." I snap my mouth shut, losing my train of thought, because I want to lie and say *no,* protest that it was wrong and that they had no right, but something won't let me.

I nod instead, sheepish.

Colt grins at me, but Wes is frowning.

"We have a problem," he says. "The kitchen is gone. And with it, our food provisions. We'll have to go hunting again, but first, we have to wait for Peter and Tink to come back."

"It's okay. I'm not that hungry," I say, my brain stalling on the 'the kitchen is gone' bit.

"You should be." Colt nods toward the house, and I assume the bedroom. "After all that sex."

"Is that what you think we did?" Heat suffuses my face. I wanted to rail at them for leaving me tied up with their guns inside of me but now I'm here, in front of them, I can't remember why.

Yes, it had made me cry. Yeah, it had humiliated me when Tink and then Peter found me like that.

But it had been so good...

"Something doesn't add up, though," Colt says. "If Peter fucked you... even if you had the necessary magic before, it must be gone now. So why is the island changing? If you were the one—and that's still up for debate—it's all over."

"*Should* be all over," Wes says.

"And we should get our turn," Colt says, his gaze darkening as it runs over me.

"Excuse me?" I breathe.

"To fuck you," he clarifies, as if that needed clarification. "With our dicks."

Okay, maybe the clarification *was* needed. "I didn't say you could," I say coolly.

"Don't lie to yourself," Wes says, now grinning, too. "You want it."

My eyes narrow. "Is that so?"

"You can't deny it."

It makes me mad, because why not? Why can't I lie to myself, or to them?

"What's with this place?" I demand. "Is lying not allowed?"

"It's Neverland," Colt says with a small shrug. "The Fae can't lie. Neither can visitors."

"But Peter did lie, didn't he? Said I wasn't the one, then said I *am* the one..."

"Peter is... special." Wes gives a shrug, too. "It's why he's the King."

"And why he can travel between worlds," I mutter.

Wes nods. "Yeah."

"Who is he really? How can he do that?"

Colt and Wes share a quick look. "He'd have to tell you that. If he decides it's important. Unless of course you go mad first."

"I won't."

Their gazes return to me, kind of blank, as if to say, *wait and see.*

Well, *shit.*

———

PETER AND TINK COME BACK HOME SOMETIME LATER, AS EVENING falls, carrying fresh kill—a few hares and birds that look like pheasants with bright green and orange plumage.

Then the Twins go to build a fire pit outside, now that we are *sans* kitchen, and they've taken a few chairs out, too.

I walk to the house door and stand there, watching them. They seem so... normal, all four of them, cozy and domestic. As if they hadn't wreaked havoc on my body and emotions scant hours ago.

And all of them obviously unfazed by the fact the house has changed. The house has risen out of the ground, and the steps leading down to the door are no more. The roof has brown tiles. The front door is painted blue, like the window shutters. So... fairytale-like, a cottage out of a children's story, and yet somehow familiar.

I shiver.

"You're wearing my T-shirt," Tink says, green eyes flicking my way. Something in them shifts, a spark jumps.

"It was the only thing I could find," I mutter. "Peter tore my clothes apart."

"He did, didn't he?" Tink tilts his head to the side, his gaze turning to Peter who is standing by the fire. Copper hair slides over his eyes.

"You're not any better," I say. "You found me with those guns stuck in me, and just left me there."

And for some reason, I expected more from Tink. Compared to Peter, or even the Twins, he'd seemed the nicer one, but now I'm not so sure. Worse still, he warned me. He told me he's not a good guy, that none of them are, so why am I having so much trouble believing it, even in the face of evidence?

"Peter sent me out, if you recall," Tink goes on.

"And what's he got on you that you can't fight back and stand your ground?"

Tink stares at me, then gives a bark of laughter. "I take it he hasn't explained about the shadows."

I lift a brow. "The shadows?"

"*Our* shadows."

"No. But..." I swallow hard. "But I thought I saw his shadow in the bedroom. I saw it moving on the walls. Independently from him."

"Right. Yeah. You saw that. So, Peter, will you tell her, or should I?"

Peter is scowling down at his hands. They're hanging between his knees. "What does it matter now?"

"Oh, I don't know," Tink says. "Maybe it doesn't. Maybe she has the right to know, since we brought her here against her will."

"You're turning soft," Peter says.

"And you're destroying everything we've been fighting for all these years."

Peter's jaw works. He doesn't deny it.

"Holy shit," Colt says, his gaze hard on Peter. "You really did fuck her. I thought Tink was exaggerating."

"I never exaggerate," Tink says.

Wes snorts. "Right..."

"Fuck this," Peter says, gets on his feet and stalks off.

I stare at his tall shape heading for the woods, not sure what set him off.

"Stay close," Tink calls after him. "Don't wander off and make me come after you."

Peter lifts his hand and gives him the finger without turning around.

"Peter!" I start after him, and Colt says something in a warning tone, something about a ritual, but I don't stop, my rushed steps turning into a jog. "Wait."

Peter is faster than I expected and as I run among the

scraggly trees, I start to panic. Where is he? I can't see him anywhere. I stop, panting, turning in a circle.

"Peter?" I call out. "Where are you?"

Silence is my only answer. A bird tweets on a tree and flies away in a flap of wings, scaring the bejesus out of me.

Okay, Dee, think. It has just belatedly occurred to me that maybe he's simply ignoring me, refusing to answer. That he doesn't want to talk to me.

Well, tough. Normally I'd give him his privacy, his space, his time, whatever he needs, but this isn't a normal situation. Peter isn't my friend, or even a nice guy. He's my kidnapper, the situation is sort of insane, and I need answers.

So, quiet as a mouse, I stalk through the trees, looking for him. Damn, but dead leaves do crunch when you step on them, no matter how careful you are. Keeping to a faint trail winding through the sparse woods, I manage to keep the noise at a minimum.

Maybe he's supernaturally fast, like a vampire or something, and he's already at the other end of the island, whatever that is—or... he's nearby.

I feel sort of ridiculous as I glance behind tree trunks in case he's there. He has shoulders like a quarterback. No tree trunk will hide him.

And yet, as I stalk deeper into the woods, I think I hear his voice threading through the trunks, even if he remains invisible.

Then I see him, at last.

He's standing in a small clearing. There's a fallen tree trunk behind him and a brook is gurgling nearby, hidden in the grass and rushes.

His head is bent, dark hair sculpted from onyx, his face hidden, broad shoulders slightly hunched. Something flashes in his hand, caught in the moonlight.

A blade.

What is he doing, what—?

He lifts the knife and runs the blade over his inked forearm. Cutting into his skin, into the designs covering it. The black ink masks the thin scars, I realize, as blood wells, looking black in the washed-out shades of the early evening, and drips to the ground.

I'm too dumb-struck to speak or make a sound as he lets his blood run. Too stunned to even wonder how the ink has returned to his skin when I could swear it wasn't there earlier.

The crimson dripping fills my vision.

The word 'ritual' is now starting to make sense, but why?

Why do this?

"I remember, Mom," he whispers, or at least that's what I think he's whispering. He lifts the blade, then points it at the ground, letting the blood drip off its tip. "Some things can't be forgotten."

I take a step back, suddenly all too aware of intruding on a personal moment—and a twig cracks under my heel.

He whips around, quick as lightning, and is on me in two strides, lifting the bloodied knife to my throat. "You!"

"Sorry, sorry!" I lift my hands, swallow. "Didn't mean to intrude. I only wanted... only wanted to talk."

He's glaring at me and for a long moment, I don't know if he really sees me, if he knows who I am.

Then he lets out a breath, lowers the blade. "Wendy."

"Oh, now you remember my name."

"Sometimes I do," he says, "and sometimes I don't."

"Because of your shadow?"

"What would you know about shadows?" His blue eyes are fixed on me, unwavering.

"That yours is monstrous."

"True," he says.

"And seems... detached from you."

"Not fully, sadly," he admits. "Though maybe it's the other way around."

"What is?"

"Not having a full shadow is... a problem."

I almost laugh. "The way I see it, you're all problematic here."

"Yeah, well..." He shrugs, frowns down at the blade in his hand. "You know now my shadow problem. But I'm not the only one. The Twins only have one shadow to share between them. And as for Tink... well, he has no shadow at all."

"What are these shadows?" I wonder. "And how is that possible? Any of that?"

"How is anything possible? It's reality."

"Is it?"

He sheathes the knife at his belt, lifts a hand to my pendant. "Why are you wearing this thing?"

"It's a thimble," I murmur, looking down at it, annoyed at the change of topic. "For sewing."

"You sew?"

"My mom used to. When I was little. It reminds me of those times, I guess. What's your pendant for?"

"Mine..." He blinks, lets his hand fall away. "Mine is a clue to who I am."

"And who are you?"

He shakes his head and looks away. "Listen..."

But he trails off, expression starting to go distant.

That's not good.

"Tell me about your shadow," I say, desperate not to let his mind drift off again. "How can it be detached from you? How can all this be true and what does it mean?"

"Fae reality is different from what you're used to. Neverland is just another word for the Otherworld. For Faerie. And the shadow is the soul, so if that is starting to make more fucking sense for you now and we're done with questions..."

"But—"

"And why the hell am I answering your questions? First, I fuck you, then I talk to you..." He's shaking his head as if his actions are incomprehensible and I feel slightly hurt that he should find it so strange that he wants me or would take the time to talk to me.

"You'd rather I left you alone to cut yourself some more?" I ask scathingly.

"I'd rather you went back to the house," he says, "and stayed there."

Well, that's a dismissal if I ever heard one.

15

WENDY

"I like it," Tink says as I walk back into the house, morose and wondering why the hell I didn't take the chance to run away instead of coming back, doing Peter's bidding.

He's standing by a fireplace that hadn't existed when I arrived. Had it been there when I'd last been inside the sitting room?

"You like what?"

He lifts a brow. "That you're wearing my clothes."

"It's only your stained T-shirt," I mutter, tugging on the hem, "since I couldn't find anything else to wear. I could hardly go around topless."

"I don't see why not." Tink winks at me—but I remember him leaning over me where I was tied to the bed, laughing at me, and my smile fades before it fully forms.

"You're aroused by us," he'd said, "you lust after us, you like us touching you, kissing you. But we never did any of that for you. Only for ourselves. For our own pleasure. Our own excitement."

"What would you rather wear, then?" Tink comes to stand beside me, resting a long-fingered hand on the mantel. "I'll find it for you."

"Find whatever I want? Like, how, are you going to snap your fingers and use magic?"

"Nah. We have a trunk full of clothes." Doubt crosses his gaze. "If it's still here. Do you want a dress?"

I shrug. "Sure. The weather is warm. A dress will do just fine."

He lift his hand off the mantel and touches my hair. A dark spark flares in his eyes. Then he turns, his hand falling away. "Stay here."

So of course I follow him—not sure what this small show of rebellion will help with, but at least it feels good—where he kneels down by a wooden, carved trunk behind the sofa.

"Aha!" He opens the lid and rummages inside. I look down at his glossy head, the dark hair and pink streaks that don't look dyed but rather like they grow like that straight from the roots, and his wide shoulders. He's still dressed in the ratty T-shirt he had on when I arrived here, long legs clad in worn jeans. "Here it is. Sometimes when the island shifts, things get lost."

"It has happened before? That the island changed?"

"Oh, yeah. We're not sure why and how, but we think maybe the island has been shaped after every Wendy's dream."

"And you said it changed now?"

"In some ways. Turned out quite well, wouldn't you say? Can't say I cared much for living underground." He pulls a wad of pink cloth out of the trunk, drops it back inside, pulls out something blue. "Maybe having sex isn't such a bad idea, if it fixes houses like that. And to think I haven't even shown you my sword yet." He winks at me as he shakes out a white dress. "What do you think?"

"About your sword?"

He laughs. Turns his head to look up at me from where he's kneeling. "Wait till you see it. It's huge."

"Do all of you have such a big ego or is it mostly you?"

"Only I have a sword," he says solemnly. "The others have

daggers, at best. They can't compare to me. It's not ego, it's a fact."

"Are we still talking about weapons?"

He returns to his rummaging with a snicker and a shrug.

"Yeah, most probably not." I sigh. "Where did you get these dresses?"

"I don't cross-dress if that's what you're thinking." He frowns. "Though I bet a dress would look good on me. I have the legs for it."

"Tink—"

"You don't think so?"

Muscular, long legs, sure, but I'm not going to play along, or compliment him and feed his ego. "Who did the dresses belong to? Did you steal them from the real world?"

"No." He shakes his head. Doesn't look up.

That's a big fat clue, right there, his refusal to meet my eyes or explain. Which means...

"They belonged to the other girls, right?" I breathe. "The ones who came before me?"

A pause. Then, "Yeah."

"What did you do with the girls? You said they jumped off the cliffs, Hook said they're buried. So which one is it?"

Tink rubs at his eyes. "Those whose bodies we retrieved are on the island. There's a cemetery with a memorial for them. We call them the Golden Girls."

"Jesus." I draw an uneven breath. I can't speak for a few beats and he also seems to fall still, as if waiting for me to go on. "There is a song about that," I say eventually, my mind going through strange leaps. "About Golden Girls."

"I bet there is," he mutters.

Golden. That reminds me of Peter's golden acorn pendant, and of my own silver thimble. I reach for it and a small gasp escapes me.

"What is it?" he asks.

"I lost... I lost my pendant. A thimble that used to belong to my mom." I look around, bend to look under the furniture. "Have you seen it?"

"Nope. Maybe it fell in the woods."

"I need to go look for it."

"Certainly not. No time for that now. I'm just going to... Ah." Tink pulls something else from the trunk—flat ballerina shoes —and rises to his feet, towering over me. He thrusts the dress and shoes at me. "Here."

Still saddened by the loss of my pendant, I look down at it without much interest. "How do you know they will fit?"

"I have a good eye for sizes. Go on, try them on."

Struggling to put out of my mind the fact that these items belonged to dead girls, dead girls who bear my name, I clutch the dress and shoes to me. "Turn around."

"What?" His dark brows draw together. "You are aware that I saw your pussy stuffed with a gun, right?"

"Thanks for reminding me," I grumble, my face suddenly too warm. "Now turn around."

I don't really expect him to obey, but he shrugs and turns his broad back to me. "Hurry up," is all he says.

"Why?"

"We're going out."

———

"GOING OUT WHERE?" I ASK AS I PUSH DOWN MY SKIRT, STANDING naked in the living room. Instinctively I put my hands over my breasts to cover them.

Which is stupid. He's not even looking.

Is he?

I don't know why I feel so vulnerable, standing without any clothes in front of him. After all, he has his back turned and like he said, he's seen it all already, but there you have it.

"It's the anniversary. There's a tradition. We go to see the mermaids dance." He turns his face to the side and winks. "You can't say we don't take you places."

"Ugh, those horrible creatures?" I lift the dress, hold it against my body. It smells of dried herbs. "Why should we watch them dance? And an anniversary of what?"

"Tonight, we have a sort of truce," Tink says, and I don't immediately see how that is an answer to my question. "An unspoken promise that we can meet under the night sky and not try to kill each other. Hook and his gang will be there, too. Even the Reds sometimes come."

"The monsters?"

"The very same."

The dress fits me fine, the hem hitting me right above the knees, the cleavage modest—which is good, since I don't have any panties, or a bra for that matter, and my boobs are not on the small side.

"I'm surprised you didn't try to sneak a look," I say as I slip my feet into the white ballerinas which, surprisingly, also fit.

"Oh, there's the mirror." Tink gestures at a mirror that again hadn't been there this morning as he turns back around.

Oh my God. It shouldn't surprise me that he was ogling me, and also it shouldn't matter, like I said before, but it still annoys me.

"You're an asshole."

"Surprised?" He grins. "Not much entertainment to be had on the island, doll. I'll get what I can."

"Before I'm gone, you mean, buried with the other Golden Girls?"

He gives a small sigh. "Nothing personal. Ready to roll?"

It's hard to stay angry. I guess, when shock after shock hits you, you quickly grow kind of numb. "Were you well entertained by me, at least?"

He tips his head back a little, observing me from under his lashes. His voice drops an octave. "I sure was."

"Well." I ignore the fresh wave of heat washing over my face and neck. I live to please, as it turns out. "Where are the others?"

"We'll meet them there."

"Which is where?" I ask. "Don't tell me on the beach."

He shoots me a quizzical look. "Well, we're going to the mermaids, so... yeah?"

"Shit." I take a calming breath. It doesn't do jack. "Shit!"

"You still haven't told me why you hate the water," he says.

"What does it matter?" I glare at him. "Apparently, we're going anyway, or is there a chance I could pass on today's anniversary celebrations?"

"No," he says. "Let's go."

———

"You still haven't told me what anniversary it is today," I say.

"Can't you guess? No?" We're walking side by side down a path through the trees, in a different direction than the town or where I'd found Peter earlier, the moon shining in the sky, and Tink... he seems to be faintly glowing in the dark. "It's Peter's birthday."

"His birthday?"

"You like repeating words I say, I see."

I huff. "But why call it an anniversary?"

"Because it's not his real birthday, of course."

"Oh, of course," I grumble. "Makes perfect sense. *Not.*"

"The anniversary of his turning," he says slowly, as if explaining things to an idiot.

Which doesn't amuse me. "Turning what?"

"Not what. *Into* what, that's what you should be asking."

I sigh. "I give. What has he turned into, then? He seems perfectly human to me." I reconsider that. "Well, apart from the wonky shadow and the fact he can travel between worlds. The fact he's a psycho falls well within human nature, I'm afraid."

Tink snorts. "Human? He hasn't been human for a very long time."

"What happened?"

Tink is silent for a while as we trudge down an incline and he helps me across a brook. I wonder if it's the same one I heard in the clearing where Peter was earlier.

"Did you know that Peter self-harms?" I ask.

"Come again?" Tink frowns.

"He uses a knife to make cuts on his arms."

"Oh. *That*."

A wave of anger hits me. "You know about it. You don't care?"

"Seriously, Wendy girl, after everything you've seen and heard, after everything that has been done to you since you arrived, this is what spooked you? We're all damaged, or haven't you noticed?"

Yeah, he's got a point. "So what is Peter?"

"Who knows?"

"Try again, Tink."

He rolls his eyes. "I guess... I guess it doesn't matter much now if you know, since you can't save us."

"So tell me."

"Well, it started with Peter and Hook. They were the first. Maybe... maybe Hook was first. They don't talk much about it. Fact is, when Peter arrived here, it seems Hook was here already."

"And they fought?"

"No. No, at first, they were friends. More than friends, if you catch my drift."

I stare at his stony, handsome profile. "Really?"

"Yeah. But Peter came here willingly. He ran from home. Whereas Hook... I heard rumors that he was taken."

"By the Fae?" I want to know.

"That's right. Peter wanted to get away. I doubt he planned to get stuck here. Bringing a human here, trying to turn him into a Fae... it drives people mad. Destroys their shadow. He's barely clinging on to his. He was chosen to be king of the island. Hook didn't like that."

"Shadow is the soul," I whisper.

He shoots me a funny look. "Where did you hear that?"

"Peter said it."

"Damn. You know what, enough of this," Tink says harshly, grabbing my arm and hurrying me down the path. "You need to stop asking so many questions."

"Because you'll lose me soon?" I ask through gritted teeth. "Because you're afraid you might like me and then watch me go mad and jump off a cliff?"

He says nothing but his jaw works and his brows draw together. He drags me along so fast I skid on the path all the way to the shore.

16

WES

The night sky is alight with shooting stars and the sea is swirling with luminescent jellyfish and strings. We're standing on the Rock gazing down at the waves. It's damn beautiful but it won't last.

The mermaids are coming.

The Reds are already there, lurking in the woods behind us, and I do my fucking best not to shake in my boots at the thought of their proximity.

This isn't a normal night, I remind myself. It's the anniversary. They will honor it.

So far, they always have. No reason why that should change. So I try to ignore the way the scars on my back hurt from the first time I was attacked by one, before I knew to never let my guard down, to have eyes on the back of my head, to not trust innocent-looking ruins.

Nightmares can spring out of anywhere on this island.

On an island already full of nightmares.

The presence of the Reds nearby always has me nervous, even with the truce. Not as nervous as the mermaids, but still, the Reds are the more immediate threat, on solid ground, always coming at us, always ready to kill.

One fucking strange thing? The Reds have faces now. And by now, I mean since Wendy arrived. Distorted and yet *human* faces.

Their parts turned to metal, too, transforming them into giant cyborgs. When the change came, we knew that a new Wendy had been born—and still we couldn't know it was the right one.

There can only be one and I never could figure out whether that meant that the rest of them were decoys for us to smash our heads against or just candidates who never reached their potential, who knows why.

Anyway, I'm on edge, my hand on the gun handle, my eyes scanning the sea, my ears straining for any sound from the woods behind us. Hook and his gang haven't shown up yet.

And then I feel her approaching.

Wendy.

Colt glances at me. He's felt it, too. Of course he has. We're linked in strange ways. Sharing a shadow means sharing all sensations, emotions, and yet...

And yet we're night and day, light and dark. He's the rough one, the unhinged one, the one who will grab a girl by the hair as I kiss her, who will fuck her ass as I caress her pussy, who will spank and lash her while I fuck her mouth.

Who do you think is the human and who is the Fae?

Go on, guess.

Sometimes I'm not even sure myself. Especially since the memories I have from my childhood are all mixed up, fuzzy and grainy like old film strips.

It isn't only Peter's memory that's affected by the island. He's just hit the worst. With great power comes great pain. And madness.

Always madness.

I turn and watch them arrive. Tink is dragging Wendy along, a thundercloud on his face, and she's...

She's beautiful.

In a short white dress, so innocent and pure even as it hugs her curves, hinting at all that is underneath. Her hair falls on her shoulders, a fall of gold, and her eyes are wide, her mouth an unhappy line.

Yeah, she's perfect.

"Is she giving you trouble?" Peter drawls, not even taking his eyes off the heaving, glowing sea.

"Screw you," she hisses, trying to yank her arm free of Tink's hold.

"Punishment will have to wait for later," Peter says.

"What do you mean? Let me go!" She kicks at Tink's shin and he curses, hauling her to the edge of the rock, where we're standing.

"Little hellcat," he mutters, coming to stand beside me.

Her cheeks are red, chest heaving. She is angry, and afraid, and confused, and my dick is so damn hard my head is spinning from all the blood rushing south.

"I'll punish her," I rasp.

"Out of the question," Tink says. "It's my turn."

Peter says nothing, so fuck, I guess it is Tink's turn. *Fucker.* I glare at him and he grins back at me, all teeth. Even half a Fae, he's got power enough to make me reconsider punching his handsome face.

Tink is... unlike any man I've ever known. Mercurial, pretty but not in a girly way, his jaw too square and his body too broad and masculine for that comparison. We've never fucked, but I can't deny I want him.

It gets lonely in between Wendies, especially with Peter gone for long periods hunting for them, and being stuck on the island means the only people I get to spend time with are Colt and Tink.

And Tink is still a mystery to me. I sometimes wonder if he has sexual urges at all or if he only feeds off violence.

He does like punishing girls. The Fae side of him craves it. Maybe almost as much as Peter craves it, though it's different. Peter is different when his shadow takes over him. His shadow changes him.

Tink is like that all the time, torn between what he craves and what his human side abhors.

Almost like me and Colt—only we are two people. His conflict rages inside of him. He's a puzzle of a man, threatening to split down the middle. Colt and me? We're already apart, and yet we keep colliding together.

"Here they come," Peter says, breaking through my spiraling thoughts, and I blink at the sea.

At first, I don't see anything out of order. The waves sparkle as they crash against the rocks, the bioluminescent spreading through the white lace of the foam. But the Reds behind us growl and rustle, and then I see them.

The mermaids are swimming toward the shore, silvery shapes breaking the waves, riding over them, slicing through them like eels, tails occasionally splashing against the surface of the water.

Their song rises, strident and yet melodious, tugging on my mind. Beckoning. Alluring and sweet, yet sharp, digging claws into my head.

I take a step closer to the edge.

Colt's hand on my shoulder yanks me back. His breathing is uneven, his eyes a bottomless dark. Does his nature give him better control when it comes to this? Or am I just too distracted?

I'm thinking too hard, that's for sure.

The mermaids are now filling the small bay, heads and torsos rising over the surface, their voices growing louder, a symphony in cacophony, a melody that is so strangely beguiling it confuses the senses, just like their appearance.

When the light strikes their faces, some look like pretty maidens and others like half-rotted corpses, their long hair green and blue and gray, flowing over youthful or sagging or skeletal bodies.

Peter gasps, leaning forward, eyes wide. The call is the strongest for him and I reach for his arm to stop him from falling, extending the favor Colt did me.

Tink is faster, grabbing him and hauling him back. He tells Peter something about getting a grip and staying strong but Peter doesn't seem to hear him.

"What sort of celebration is this, anyway?" Wendy demands, her voice barely audible over the howl of the mermaid song. "I don't like it."

Who does? It's not a celebration but a commemoration, but it doesn't matter either way.

We're not here by choice.

The mermaids sing and sing, and we struggle against the pull of their voices. At some point, I notice Hook and his pirate gang. They're standing some distance back, on the rock behind us.

At least, if the Reds decide to attack, they'll snack on them first.

"The Reds won't attack," Colt says with that uncanny ability of his to read my mind at odd moments. "It's truce day."

"Yeah, yeah," I mutter, returning my attention to the sea. "As you say."

Then there's nothing more to say because the Mermaid Queen shifts and stands in the shallows on long, pale legs. She is naked, long green hair spilling over her shoulders, her back, and her breasts like a cape. A crown of red coral gleams on her head and her eyes glow like searchlights.

Unnerving.

"Peter Pan!" she calls out, lifting a hand, as if in greeting. An ancient goddess of the sea. A fey creature, one of the rulers of Faerie—and she's been set on Peter since he appeared on the scene of the world.

"Mermaid Queen," he says, not shouting and yet his voice carries over the wind. The song of the mermaids has ceased, at least.

"Have you reconsidered? Will you join us? Will you be our king?"

Peter draws a breath that's strangely loud and shakes his head. "I won't."

"What is holding you back? Soon your mind will be all gone. Anything that ties you to the human world will have faded. You still haven't found the right girl to break the spell. You never will."

"You don't know that," Peter says.

"The girl beside you," the Queen says. "She's as empty of magic as a broken cup trying to contain the ocean. Give her to me and free yourself."

"No," Wendy whispers, her face gone white, "no!"

How isn't she caught by the Queen's spellbinding voice?

"I keep telling him that," Hook's voice echoes. "To give up. Join us."

"James," the Queen says. "James Hook. The Beautiful One. The Terrible One. We brought you here and you're loyal to us to the end. Keeping Neverland safe from the human world incursions. Keeping the nightmares at bay."

"My Queen." Hook bows deep, silver hair sliding forward to hide his face.

Hook is another mystery, a deeper one. Gorgeous like an angel, a traitorous bastard who will battle us at every turn of the way—when we find a Wendy who might save us, when we lower our defenses, when we try to leave the island.

He hates us.

The Queen has given him a gift—that thrice-damned watch he is wearing, a magical tool that protects his mind from Neverland's magic.

So he doesn't forget.

Isn't going mad.

Unlike us.

Which means he has no excuses for being such an asshole. No good excuses, anyway.

I wonder what he's getting out of this. Gold? A retirement plan? A magic reservoir to use once the rest of us have gone mad?

No, he probably wants to be king instead of Peter. Hoping to convince the Queen to step in, once Peter is gone and—

A scream shatters the night, and I draw my gun before my mind catches up with whatever the fuck is going on. Hissing growls and more screams—and fuck me, I hate it when my fears are realized.

"The Reds!" I yell, hating the terror gripping me, the 'I-told-you-so' clogging my throat. "They're attacking!"

"What the hell." Colt has already drawn his gun and is squinting at the woods behind us. "It's supposed to be a fucking truce!"

Peter snarls, raising his knives, but it's his shadow that's his greatest weapon, expanding behind him like a black mantle.

Tink has grabbed Wendy's arm again, his sword shining in his other hand.

"What have you done?" Hook roars. "Peter, what the fuck have you done?"

"Fuck off, James." Peter breaks into a run toward the woods. "It wouldn't surprise me if this was your doing."

"Only the true Wendy could break such a spell," Hook says, "the spell of the truce," and it gives me pause.

"But Peter has already fucked her!" Tink growls as he drags Wendy behind him, the Reds loping toward us, claws and fangs, rusty metal and rows of shark-like teeth in faces that look disturbingly human.

"Maybe the magic changed," I yell as I lift my gun, take aim and fire. A Red drops to the ground, twitching. "You said the island is changing. How would that be possible if she wasn't the one?"

"Your guess is as good as mine," Tink says.

"Wes!" Colt shoves me out of the way and shoots one, two, three bullets into a massive Red that skids by, then drops off the cliff into the sea. "Dammit."

"Yeah. We have to go." My fucking heart is slamming about inside my chest. "Let's go!"

"No shit. Peter!" Colt hollers, shooting at another Red coming at us, lifting a handful of bullets from his pocket. "We'll be your distraction. Go!"

No, he's not sacrificing himself to save Peter. Don't mistake this for the sign of a soft heart. Colt is nothing if not pragmatic. Peter is the king and he has Wendy, who may or may not be the one who will save us, so we have to protect them.

We're Peter's bodyguards of sorts and we work great together as a team. Almost like real Twins.

I don't know if Peter hears Colt's shout, but Tink seems to, grabbing both and hauling them toward the west.

"Go!" Colt shouts at me and I start shooting as we run the other way, down the Rock, felling Red after Red as we skid and slide down to the beach.

We won't make it. The Reds have gathered in mass. Killing one of them is hard and messy. Killing hundreds of them?

Impossible.

We're going to die, shredded apart and probably eaten, too.

Not the best way to go.

Grabbing bullets from my pocket, I reload my gun as we run, stumbling over rocks. Mermaids are crawling up the beach, clawed hands reaching for us. One grabs my ankle and I almost go down, managing to stay on my feet at the last moment.

Yanking my leg free, I resume running. My ankle burns. The Reds are thumping down the beach toward us.

Colt turns and fires.

I turn to do the same, lifting my gun, but I don't fire, because... "What in the nine circles of hell?"

Hook's gang is fighting the Reds, forming a river between us and the monsters, flowing into the Reds' mass, hacking them down. They are eerily quiet as they do so, the only noise coming from the Reds who roar and growl and howl.

What is Hook doing? Has he finally lost his mind, too?

"Hook!" I shout. "Hook! What the fuck?"

"Run!" he yells at us, swinging his cutlass, the curved blade flashing through the night as he cuts a Red's arm off. "Run for your lives!"

Colt glances at me. "But you... you're on the mermaids' side! The Reds do their bidding."

"I never had anyone complain to me for saving their life before," Hook says, just loud enough to be heard, a wry note in his voice.

"I don't trust this," I mutter.

"Not all forms of slavery look the same," Hook says, loping off a Red's head.

"What is that supposed to mean?"

Hook shoots me a bleak look and doesn't reply, turning to hack at another monster, his men swarming out of the woods to his aid.

So we run.

―――

WE RUN AND RUN, AND WHEN WE STOP TO CATCH OUR BREATH, and Colt grabs me and shoves me against a tree trunk, slamming my back against the rough bark.

He kisses me.

It's as aggressive and violent as he is. He always looks like the thoughtful one, the careful and gentle one, but once he unleashes himself, once his control snaps, he's like a storm rushing over the land.

Over people.

I kiss him back, needing the release as much as he does.

Listen, we're not brothers, even if they call us the Twins. He's my changeling. And I am his. I may never know which way it went—who stole one child and replaced it with the other.

It doesn't even fucking matter anymore.

All the anticipation of the past years and months turning into bitter disappointment once more, all the lust and craving for this new girl that we weren't allowed to fuck, all this fear and frustration and inner fight setting us on edge again and again and again... it has to find an outlet, sooner or later.

And while I'm more into girls, and Wendy is like a hot dessert I can't wait to dive into, ticking all my boxes, triggering all my wants, a hot boy will do in a pinch.

Not just any hot boy.

This one.

Whipcord muscle, big capable hands, a square jaw, a face like a painting by the old masters, one of those Old Testament angels coming to warn Job or whoever it was of the end of the world.

I tangle my fingers in his long, dark hair, tug until he snarls and bites my lower lip, sucking it between his teeth.

Pain for pain. Grip for grip. His hand grabs the back of my head, angles it so he can deepen the kiss.

This is just relief, I tell myself. Nothing else, nothing more, ever. That's our mutual understanding. Sexual relief, a flash of blinding pleasure, a moment to let ourselves go before we snap.

I like the scrape of the rough bark against my back, scratching at my skin through my shirt. I like Colt's strength, his barely leashed aggression. I like that he doesn't hold back with me.

He probably doesn't hold back with anyone.

His chest presses against mine and our cocks grind together through the rough fabric of our pants, hard, unyielding poles. The pleasure, though expected, startles the fuck out of me and I cry out in his mouth.

Too much pent-up need.

His answering groan tells me he feels the same way.

He breaks the kiss and uses both hands to tear my pants open and yank them down, and I fight him to unbuckle his belt and return the favor. He helps me, a low growl showing his displeasure at the delay.

That's how we are when this happens. Impatient. Rushing. Racing toward the end, never stopping to savor it.

Then again, to be fair, it usually happens on the heels of a bad event flooding us with adrenaline, stiffening our dicks, getting us hard and aching. It's never something to ease ourselves into. It's something to get ourselves out of.

"Fuck," he breathes, slamming our bared dicks together, rubbing against me, his hand sliding back up my neck, my throat, gripping my jaw. "Oh, fuck..."

Groaning, I let my head fall back. Why is this such fucking bliss, to thrust against another hard cock, to have a muscular chest pressed to mine? I like many things, I guess, various things. Both soft and hard, both girls and boys.

Above all... I'll take what I can get. This is the most gentleness I've ever had, and Colt doesn't know this, probably wouldn't give a damn, but it's a drug, being held, being touched, like now, when his hold on my jaw relaxes a little and his thumb brushes over my skin.

Hot damn...

It's over quickly. I snap my hips against him, one of my hands leaving bruises on his hip, the other on his shoulder, and the pressure crests, bursting. My dick jerks, spattering our chests with white ropes of cum.

Colt breathes a curse, bows his head and then he's coming, too, his cum crosshatching mine. Long strands of dark hair stick to his sweaty neck and face, his lashes are black fans on his sharp cheekbones. I can't help it.

I kiss him again.

His mouth crashes against mine, no hint of softness, though his thumb keeps caressing my cheek. His lashes don't lift and his eyes... they look soft and unguarded, hazy.

It doesn't last.

Then he's pulling back already, like every time, his gaze sharpening. "We should get going. See if the others made it back okay."

He's right. Colt is not only the violent side of me, he's also the voice of reason. Don't ask how the two mix. It's one of life's great mysteries.

He's right, anyway, so we head home.

17

WENDY

These people are off their rockers.

Placing themselves between cannibal mermaids and nightmarish monsters? Oh, and doing so alongside their sworn enemy gang, hoping nobody will change their mind and attack?

And oh boy, did they attack.

The monsters did, that is.

Having the gall to look surprised, Tink hauls me away from the rock and the beach, heading back into the woods while the Twins lead the monsters away.

I try not to worry that we won't make it, that the Twins won't make it, that some of the monsters will notice the ruse and come our way, that the mermaids can shapeshift like their queen and walk on dry land, pick us up one by one and snack on us.

What's stopping them, right? Something's got to be stopping them or everyone on the island would be history by now.

Unless, like Tink said, the island is changing... But nobody batted an eye when the Queen shifted, so I guess that was normal?

Jesus, I don't know what to think anymore. I don't know what I know. It's like being dropped on another planet and trying to figure it all out without a manual and special black-ops training.

"Pick up your pace," Tink hisses. My arm hurts where he's gripping me, his fingers like steel, digging into my flesh. "We're not out of the woods yet."

"The house *is* in the woods."

"I was figuratively speaking," he snaps. "Where is Peter? Peter!"

With a roar, Peter slams himself into a tree, then takes two steps back and does it again.

And again.

"What the fuck?" Tink drags me over even though I dig my heels in, trying to hang back. He grabs Peter's shoulder. "Stop!"

Blood is running down Peter's face. He blinks at Tink as if he doesn't know him, then blinks again and I see horror dawning on his face.

It's gone in a flash.

Or maybe I was wrong. After all, though the sky is still raining stars, it's quite dark under the sparse foliage.

It's impossible not to notice, though, that Tink keeps his grip on Peter's shoulder as we trudge down the path and that Peter allows it as if he isn't too sure he can stay on his feet, or on the path, without help.

"What happened?" I demand, now that the woods are quiet and I don't hear anything trampling the undergrowth. "I thought you said it would be safe, that it's this... anniversary thing."

"It is. It was supposed to be," Tink says through gritted teeth. "Fuck, I still don't know what happened."

"You were too trusting," I mutter. "Never trust the monsters."

"I should print that on a T-shirt," Tink mutters back.

"It's her," Peter says and his voice is slightly slurred.

"Are you drunk?" I demand. "Or stoned? Maybe you're high. What did you smoke?"

He ignores me. Staggers a little. "The Twins."

"They'll be all right," Tink says.

"Against all of the Reds and the mermaids?" Peter sounds angry.

"A little late to think of them now," Tink grinds out, "but for what it's worth, I saw Hook's gang get between the Twins and the Reds."

Peter blinks. "What? Why?"

"Maybe Hook grew a conscience overnight?" Tink suggests. "What do you think?" When Peter doesn't reply, he sighs. "Yeah, too implausible. Maybe the anniversary magic still works on him, making him an ally just for tonight?"

"That's more probable," Peter agrees, rubbing at his forehead and groaning.

What a nonsensical, surrealist twist in a nonsensical, surrealist world. I feel like Alice in Wonderland, only the cute animals are crazed, sexy dudes.

"Why are you enemies with Jas?" I ask.

"Oh, are you on a first-name basis with Hook, now?" Tink whistles. "What aren't you telling us?"

"Be serious for once," I snap.

"Ow." Tink winces. "Not you, too. Peter's been rubbing off on you and not in a sexy way."

"Shut up, Tink," Peter mutters. "And as for Hook... for Jas... I thought you knew by now. He wants the throne."

"But you won't give it up?" I hazard.

He sighs. "I would if I could. *They* made me into their king.

And I can't fucking escape. A king. *Ha.* 'Pan.' You know? Like *pantheon*, like *pandemic*, like *panorama*."

"Like *panetone*," Tink supplies, hauling us both along. "And *panties*."

Peter ignores him. "Pan. It means *everything*. King of everything and nothing, King of now and never. A prisoner."

"And who is 'they'?" I whisper.

"The Dark Fae. Lords of the otherworld. Masters of nightmares." He shrugs as we stumble down the path. "The ones who invited me here, who raised me."

So I ask the logical thing. "If you are their king, how come you're a prisoner?"

"I pissed them off."

"Really?" I almost sigh. "How strange. How?"

"I tried to kill them."

That's a fun twist. "What, all of them?"

"The one who had me in his clutches."

"Not a smart move," I murmur.

"Pain drives you mad sometimes," Tink says.

I turn to him. "Pain?"

"I'm not Fae," Peter says. "This place hurts."

"Is that why the other Wendies went mad?"

He shrugs. "You will follow them soon enough."

"Great." I roll my eyes, fighting a twitch of fear. "Shouldn't I be feeling pain then?"

"You don't?" Tink whispers. His brows go up. "Wendy..."

They both stop and stare at me.

I stare back. "Should I be?"

"Damn." Tink starts walking again, pulling us along, his expression closing up. "Come on."

"She doesn't feel it," Peter is whispering, like a lost child. "She doesn't—"

"After everything, that shocks you?" Tink snaps, anger in his voice, as if he hadn't been staring at me, dumbfounded, mere seconds ago. "You keep saying she is the one and then that she isn't. You forbid us to touch her, then fuck her. The anniversary truce was broken for the first time in centuries. Doesn't that tell you something?"

"You tell me. I thought maybe I'm dreaming," Peter says. "Or hallucinating. Wouldn't be the first time. Maybe I'm in my bed at the house, imagining I found a pretty girl who can change everything."

"But you're not," Tink says, "and as for what she can do... nobody yet knows."

———

"No, you can't!" I fight Tink with all I have but his strength is a hundred times mine. "You can't tie me up on the bed again!"

"Watch me."

"Why, Tink?"

"I'm beat," he says, his voice flat. "Can't be running around in the night, looking for you, searching for your remains and having to wonder if it was a mermaid or a Red that ate you."

"I won't run."

"No, now you won't, because you won't be able to, all tied up as you are." He leans over me, licks his lips, his gaze traveling over my dress, my body. "I guess it's a free for all now. Yes, I am talking about you."

"I'm not!"

He lifts a dark brow. "Why, don't you like the thought of all four of us fucking you?"

I lick my dry lips. "Is that your way of punishing me?"

"Whether you're the right girl or not, we can't get attached to you. So we have to punish you," he'd said.

"It's a way of pleasing myself," he says.

"You're selfish."

A shrug. "I'm Fae."

"Half-Fae."

His gaze darkens. "And you're a stupid girl."

"Am I now?"

"You can't help us. Never could. And Peter is all caught up in you that he forgets himself."

"He forgets a lot of things," I whisper.

"And the Twins," he goes on as if he hasn't heard me. "They're troubled."

"Oh, is that what we're calling psychos now? Men who fuck a woman with their guns? *Troubled*?"

"I'm not talking about that." He waves a slim hand.

"What then?"

"The way they act around you. So... careful."

I stare at him. "Careful? This is their *careful*? What do they normally do?"

He snorts. Says nothing.

I try a different tack. "Please, Tink." I don't even know why I'm asking him. He's an ass. "Please, let me go. I want to go home. I have to."

Still silent, he turns to go.

"You said it yourself so many times," I call after him. "I can't help you!"

"It's not decided yet. You do... strange things to this island. Maybe you just need training."

"You mean punishment?"

"Sometimes," he says darkly, the edge of a grin in his voice, "they're one and the same."

————

He closes the door behind him as he leaves and silence spreads in the room. I tug on my bonds, my wrists chafing, but nothing gives.

I roll my head to the side. So tired. The night is rising around me, rolling over the windows. Sleep rushes over me like dark water. I thought I wouldn't be able to sleep after everything that has happened, but my body and mind are hanging on by a hair and will have to let go.

I slip into deep, right into the black water that haunts my memories. The cold grips me instantly, inside and out, and I'm shivering, flailing, screaming in the water.

Shapes flash in the deep, reaching for me, and I struggle harder.

But then... something catches my ankle and yanks, and suddenly all the fight drains out of me.

This time, I let myself go. I don't fight it anymore.

I let myself sink into the dark water.

Down and down I go, past kelp forests and rockeries, past coral walls and silvery shoals of fish. I feel the sea shift around me, the memory changing—and then I'm not being dragged down but up, toward the surface, a hand gripping my wrist instead of my ankle.

I'm lifted up into the light and a familiar face leans over me.

"Wendy?"

I think it's Peter at first—it's Peter I expected to see for some weird reason, pulling me out of the water—but it's actually Colt.

I jerk back but I'm still tied to the bed, my heart thudding. "What do you want?"

Morning is dawning outside, I realize, light spilling through the slats of the window. Behind Colt, I see Wes. I don't think I've ever seen them apart.

They both gaze down at me, eyes dark and lips parted.

I take a deep breath, trying to slow my racing pulse. "Untie me, Colt."

"I think he likes you tied up," Wes says with a grin.

"It seems you all do." My mouth is bone dry. "What about what *I* want?"

"I know what you want," Colt says and climbs onto the bed.

"Not your gun." I shake my head, my heart thumping. "Colt, no."

"Relax." Up close, he smells of cordite and sex, sweet and smoky and musky. "I've used my gun enough for one day already. Shot all those Reds down."

"Colt," I start again, but he has spread my legs and buried his face between them. Since I was never given any panties to wear, his mouth is right on my spread, bare pussy.

Whatever words were about to spill from my lips—another demand for him to untie me—are lost in a moan when his tongue flickers over my clit, then stabs into me.

"God..." I arch on the bed, twisting my hands in their bonds, as he tortures me deliciously, licking at me like a big cat, long swipes of his rough tongue, each one bringing me closer to a precipice I hadn't anticipated reaching so fast.

I moan, twist, lift my hips, trying to get more pressure, more friction where I'm burning—

And Wes shoves Colt aside, tumbling him onto the bed. "My turn." He spreads my legs more, flickers his tongue over my clit, circles it.

He presses his lips there and sucks.

Jesus.

He sucks and teases and sucks some more, taking me right there, to the very edge—and then pulls back.

"Please," I gasp, "oh God, please—"

"Fuck." Wes fumbles with his fly, frees his cock and settles between my legs.

The head of his cock nudges at my entrance, then pushes into me in one long thrust, making me cry out in shock but also relief. He's bowed over me, bright blond hair falling in his eyes, gaze intense, burning, focused on my lips.

Just when I think he's going to kiss me, Colt comes to stand beside the bed, freeing his hard cock. Even as Wes' cock fills me up so completely, I can hardly breathe, the sight of Colt's cock makes my mouth water.

"Open up like a good girl," he growls. "Take it. Take it all."

And I do. God help me, I do, and I love it, even as I choke on his fat girth. Salt and musk fill my senses as his swollen, hard flesh fills my mouth. It's an echo of when they fucked me with their guns, I realize, and yet it's so different, and *oh God...*

Is it wrong to be so wet and aching because two hot guys are using me at the same time for their pleasure? It is wrong to like it so much?

Is it wrong to feel the pleasure rush through me as I give head to Colt and get fucked by Wes, both of them grunting as they thrust into me?

My eyes roll back in my head a little as I start to come and Colt grunts, his cock jerking inside my mouth. Hot, salty cum spills down my throat, and I choke as more pleasure rushes through me.

Wes yells something I can't make out through the rushing of blood in my ears and I'm still swallowing Colt's release when Wes slams into me once, twice, hard enough to bruise, and gasps.

Marked twice.

By the time they both pull out of me, dark spots dance in my vision and my bound wrists burn almost as much as my well-used pussy, but through the deafening sound of my pulse inside my head, I hear a dark chuckle.

"I came to offer breakfast," Tink says, "but I see that's been taken care of already. Maab's tits, you guys are sick. Get off her before Peter sees you."

"I thought I was a free for all," I mutter.

"Not until Peter officially says so."

18

WENDY

"Sick," Tink repeats, eyeing all three of us, making no move to untie me. "Honestly, I've never seen you guys like this."

"You do remember we're not really brothers, right?" Wes says.

"Even so."

Wes scowls. "What, you think you're normal? Why, because you wear ripped T-shirts and jeans, trying to pass for human?"

"No, not human. But I *am* normal."

"You're half-Fae, Tink. You're as far from normal as you could possibly be."

"Says the changeling."

"Hey." I glare at all three of them. "Enough talking. Will someone finally free me?"

I can't feel my hands. I'm lying there on my back, my dress rucked up all the way to my waist, exposed, the evidence of Wes' release leaking out of me, but somehow, I don't care.

Correction, I don't care enough to be embarrassed.

Truth be told, I'm sort of... pleased. And I try not to think too hard about what that says about me, though it's obvious.

I'm not a good girl. Never was. This unexpected trip to this island from hell showed me just who I am.

A slut. A slut for these cruel, strange, gorgeous guys, a slut for punishment and sex.

And here I am, dressed in pure white like a bride, tied to the headboard of the bed, waiting to see if they feel like releasing my bonds.

Wes is the one who comes to untie the rope and unwind it from around my wrists. His golden eyes are thoughtful. "You okay?"

"Now he asks," I mutter, but I nod, rubbing at my reddened wrists. "What happened? How did you escape? Did the Reds lose you?"

"Hook intervened," he says, his gaze sliding from my face to my wrists and then to my still exposed nether regions.

Hastily, I close my legs and pull down the hem of my dress. A foolish gesture, probably. An instinctive one. He's not only seen it all already, he's tasted it and then filled it up, but... "Since when is Hook your ally?"

"Since yesterday, it seems." Wes looks away, his golden eyes troubled. "Probably just for yesterday."

"So then his alliance is already over," Tink says, sounding bored. Yet when I glance at him, his eyes are very bright and the pink in his hair has darkened to purple. "Did he say anything to you?"

"Something about slavery," Wes says.

"Not all forms of slavery look the same," Colt says.

"Meaning?" Tink frowns.

"No idea," Colt says. "That's what Hook said, is all."

"Oh." Tink's green gaze moves to me as I swing my legs off the bed and sit there, trying to catch my breath. Thoughts pass behind the mirror of his eyes like shadows. "He did, huh?"

"Where is Peter?" I ask.

"Funny you should ask that," Tink says.

"Is it?"

Tink watches me from under his lashes. "He was asking for you. Which is why I came to check."

"I thought you came to offer breakfast." I hold his gaze.

"That, too. If you're still interested..." He waves a hand negligently in the air and turns to go. "Come. I hope you like eggs. You've had sausage already."

———

"WHERE IS PETER'S FAVORITE PLACE TO EAT?" COLT SAYS.

I stare at him. "Where?"

"Wendy's, of course." His face is deadpan and I just keep staring.

Nobody laughs.

"Sit," Tink says. "Don't be shy."

"I thought you said you didn't cook," I say, sitting down at a long dining table. It looks like the kitchen didn't come back during the night. I don't remember this dining room at all.

"I said didn't want to cook," Tink says loftily. "There's a huge difference."

"Generally, he doesn't want to do anything," Wes says.

Tink doesn't deny it. He dishes out over-easy eggs into chipped colorful dishes.

"Did you cook outside?" I ask.

"In the fireplace," he says. "Flashed right back to my childhood."

"Why would you cook in fireplaces when you were little?" I ask him, curious.

"Because Neverland, or Faerie, as you mortals call it, is a pre-technological place. Or should I say a-technological? Machines don't work here. Magic jams them."

"But a stove isn't always electric," I insist. "It can work with gas, or even with coal, and—"

"Why do I bother? Eat up," is all Tink says and walks out of the house, his shoulders stiff.

"What did I say now?" I mutter, poking at my eggs. "You'd think I insulted him. He's so prickly."

"The Fae are like that," Colt offers.

I lift a brow at him. "Like what? Assholes?"

Wes snickers.

"Proud," Colt says.

"What does pride have to do with it?"

"The Fae don't like mongrels," Colt says. "So they cast him out, into the human world. But as it turns out, humans like Fae mongrels even less."

"What do you mean?" A horrible suspicion is starting to form in my mind, sending cold shivers down my spine. "What did they do to him?"

"Exposed him. Just like they'd do with a changeling. Left him in the wilderness, to see if he'd survive."

"But that's barbarous," I breathe. "And it's not done anymore."

"No? Do you know how old Tink is?"

I open my mouth, shut it. Consider this. "Very old, I assume?"

"You assume right."

"What happened then?"

"He barely made it. A wolf took him in a pack. He grew up as one of the pack. But eventually, he came across a community living in the woods."

"Hippies?"

"No, I believe it was a monastic order. Monks," he clarifies, when I stare at him. "A monastery."

"I know what a monastic order is. Tink grew up with monks? In the woods? In the mortal world?"

"That sums it up," Colt says, looking satisfied with himself.

"Well, after he was kicked out of Faerie, of course, and when he was already a teenager, I believe."

"And how did he end up back here? With all of you?"

"It's a long story," Wes says. "All our stories are long, given that we have lived long lives."

"And not boring ones," Colt supplies.

Right.

"And you..." I look at Wes who is grinning at me, a boyish grin, eyes bright, blond hair tousled and falling on his forehead. "You're that old, too?"

"Ah-huh."

"You are the changeling," I mutter. "Tink said so."

Wes' smile slips. "Perhaps."

"Meaning?"

He glances at Colt who shrugs. "One of us is. Has to be. But we both grew up in the mortal world."

"That doesn't make any sense," I say, trying to work it out. "A changeling is left by the fairies to replace a human child they take away."

"Well, someone's plans went awry," Wes says, his mouth twisting, "because when I was a baby... my parents found another baby on their doorstep. Identical to me."

"But you are..." I gesture between them. "Your colors..."

"Back then, we were both dark-haired and tawny-eyed," Wes says. "Two identical babies. Like twins. Only my mother had only had one baby. And when the maid brought the baby inside—"

"*Maid*?" I huff. "When were you born? And how rich is your family?"

"—and placed it beside the other baby, then undressed both and bathed them... she could no longer tell them apart."

"Wait." I shake my head. "Wouldn't the changeling have pointed ears, like a fairy?"

"The whole point is for the human parents to accept the

changeling as their own child. If the baby had pointed ears, that would be missing the point, wouldn't it? Pun intended."

"Right..." I put my fork down, look at their handsome faces, their closed-off expressions. "So you grew up together. Brothers if not in blood."

Colt says, "For a while. After our mother went crazy, we were passed around foster families and halfway homes. I ran away and found my way to Neverland."

"Way before me," Wes continues the tale. "He came for me later."

"I shouldn't have waited that long," Colt says, his voice low. "But time runs differently here. Or maybe it's just our damn perception that slows down. I hadn't realized. I hadn't realized many things."

"Like how fucking bad things would be here," Wes says. "Worse than in the human world."

"But the human world fucked you up." Colt is glaring at his plate as if it has offended him personally.

"Fucked us both up. Neverland finished the job." Wes grins but it's as unlike the grin from before as day from night. That grin was carefree. This one is sharp and bitter. "So, eat up, precious, before breakfast gets cold. You need to appreciate the small pleasures."

"Even if you're going mad," I whisper.

"Are you?"

I stare at their earnest gazes and wonder just how badly life has screwed these beautiful men up. "I believe Peter doesn't think I'm going mad after all."

Not that I'm sure it's true, or even that I understood right, but their eyes widen, brows arching.

"You mean you're staying?" Wes asks, a breathlessness to his voice I don't know how to interpret.

"Not dying?" Colt asks, his voice going husky.

"Um." I glance from one to the other. "Maybe... not?"

They both open their mouths to say or ask more, cheeks flushing, eyes sparkling. They look... happy?

But just then Peter walks in the door, his broad shoulders filling the opening, hands stuffed in his pant pockets, black hair sticking out in every which direction, as if he spent all night pulling on it.

His white shirt is streaked with dirt and what looks like blood, the sleeves rolled up over inked, corded forearms.

And I'm staring.

Of course I am.

"Come," he says, coming and grabbing my wrist, breaking the spell. "I need to show you something."

"Hey." I struggle against him. "What's wrong with you? You can't haul me around like this all the time."

He blinks. His lashes are very long for a guy, and his blue eyes are ridiculously pretty. "No?"

"No. Ask me to come with you and I will."

"You will?"

He sounds so confused I almost laugh. "Yes."

He frowns down where his hand is wrapped around my wrist. "I like holding you," he says. "Come."

Like a child, I think, *used to getting his own way.*

But his hold is gentle this time as he pulls me to my feet and his gaze moves over my face to focus on my lips.

"You smell like them," he mutters, his pupils dilating and before I figure out if he's angry, sad or pleased, he hauls me out of the house.

———

We walk in silence for quite a while. I feel light-headed. I have barely slept or eaten since I got here, and the path he's taking me on seems endless.

Finally, I tug back. "Can we stop for a bit?"

I don't expect him to say yes but he stops. "You okay?"

The question catches me off guard. "Yeah. Tired."

"Did the Twins fuck you too hard?"

Familiar heat seeps into my face. "None of your business."

He lifts a hand and grips my chin, eyes narrowed. "It is my business. Whatever goes on here has to do with me."

"So they fucked me with your permission?"

"Yeah."

I blink at him. "Fuck you."

His sudden grin catches me off guard. "Later. Now rest." He releases my chin, turns away and pulls something from his pocket. A click, and then the scent of fresh tobacco. Smoke curls over his head.

I lean against a trunk, watching him smoke.

"Were you fucking with me?" he asks after a moment. "You'd come if I called for you?"

I shrug. "If you asked nicely."

"I don't do nice."

"I noticed."

He walks a few paces away from me, smoking, and I think of Charlie and my brothers, waiting for me in my world. Charlie at least must be worried by now. My brothers won't notice until it's time for my weekly check-in call.

"Smoking is bad for you," I say automatically, thinking of a time Charlie had smoked after breaking up with her boyfriend. She never told me the details. Too painful, she'd said.

"So is drinking," Peter says. "And jumping between worlds. It kills you in the end."

"Are you dying?"

He shrugs. "Probably."

I glare at the back of his head. "Now you're the one screwing with me."

"No." He says it so matter-of-factly, emotionless.

Accepting it.

And I shouldn't care if it's true. Maybe I should be even glad, but I'm not and for some reason, I feel my eyes grow hot.

I start, "Peter—"

"The island has changed."

"You've said that before. What does it mean? Changed like the house? Are all the kitchens on the island gone?"

He turns to face me, blows out smoke. One corner of his mouth twitches, as if he's not sure if to smile or not. As if he has forgotten how to smile at all.

"Is it a good or a bad change?" I ask. "Will you at least tell me that?"

He seems to be considering his answer. "The Reds acquired faces right before you arrived," he says. Not the answer I expected. "Did you notice them? Recognize them?"

"No. Should I?"

He puffs out more smoke. "Pay attention next time."

"Sure, I'll make certain to take a close look as I run for my life."

His mouth does that twitching thing again.

"But that's not what you meant when you said the island is changing, is it?" I mutter.

"No."

I nod. Square my shoulders. "I've rested enough." Stepping up to him, I take the cigarette from his long fingers and throw it down. Step on it. "Lead the way."

He stares at me, brows lifting. I don't know why I'm not afraid of him right now. With a small harrumph, he turns to go, reaching for my hand as he does so.

My hand, not my wrist, I can't help but notice, tangling our fingers together.

Even less scary, he's still intimidating. Tall, broad-shouldered, his arms muscular, his strides long. The ink on the back of his hand resembles a snake's fanged mouth, dripping poison.

This is the man who kidnapped you, I remind myself. *Who tied you to the bed and fucked you there. Then gave permission to his friends to do the same.*

Whether you liked it or not is not the point.

Isn't it, though?

No, I tell myself firmly, *it isn't. You should be afraid, Wendy. You should be very afraid.*

19

WENDY

"What am I looking at?" I ask.

We're standing on a white cliff over the sea. The sun is wreathed in red and orange clouds, gilding the waves. In the distance, I think I see dolphins jumping.

Or maybe it's mermaids. Hard to tell.

"This cliff," Peter says, toying with the golden acorn hanging around his neck. It's the most nervous gesture I've ever seen him make so far. I wonder if smoking is another nervous tick.

"What about it?" I glance down and take a step back. Jesus, it's high. That's a long fall down to the water.

"This cliff wasn't here yesterday."

"It wasn't?" I try to wrap my head around this. "So what was here then? Did we have an earthquake?"

"We don't get earthquakes in Neverland. And here used to be a hunters' hut with a black door. The shore was about a kilometer away, and there was a—"

"Pier," I say automatically, "a small floating pier. Very old."

"I think so, yeah." He's frowning at me. "You know the place."

"My father..." I have to stop and swallow hard. "My father used to take us there sometimes. Me and my brothers."

"Does it have a special significance for you?"

It's my turn to frown at him. "You could say that."

The place of my worst nightmare, now washed away into nothingness. Peter doesn't remember it? Maybe it wasn't really him who pulled me out of the water?

"You have to face your fears," he says. "Those who fear are lost. Do you know what fears are?"

"What do you mean?"

"Fears are the things you avoid," he explains. "Once you've faced them, they are just problems."

"That's simplistic," I whisper.

"It's realistic. And problems can be hard to solve, too."

"Oh come on, Peter. What do you expect me to do with this bit of wisdom? What does this all mean?"

"It means that the island is growing smaller," he says. "Your nightmares are eating at Neverland. Growing bigger. Stronger. Any idea why?"

"Beats me. All of this does. Sometimes I wonder if I'm dreaming. You did say my dreams shaped this place. But I wonder if it's all in my head."

"Would you have dreamed up an asshole like me?" he growls.

"Good point. But then, what's happening? If this is all real... Why is the island changing?"

"Because *you* are changing? How the fuck should I know?" He's rubbing at the back of his neck, a faraway look in his blue eyes.

"How am I changing?"

"You tell me."

"I don't know." I frown at the sea churning below. "I don't feel any different. Have more things changed?"

"Smaller things," he admits. He sounds weary. Exhausted.

For the first time since he brought me to this island, since I woke up to find him unconscious on the beach, I study his face, the dark crescents under his eyes, the lines of tiredness at the corners of his mouth, the pale cheeks.

"Like what?"

"The geography is changing though it's nothing major. Woods turning to fields. Houses rising where before there was nothing. Parts of the town crumbling. Any idea what it might mean?"

"No. If... if this goes on," I gesture at the sea, "what happens then?"

"You mean after the sea has taken over? What do you think?"

"We'll sink and be eaten by mermaids?" I suggest.

"Probably. Unless there's a miracle."

I open my mouth to ask what sort of miracles would be necessary to stop this dark magic—my darkest memories coming to life only to be swallowed by the one element I fear the most—the water, the sea—when there's a crash behind us.

Peter turns, drawing his knives, his cigarette falling forgotten to the ground, and I spin with him, my heart pounding.

"Is it the Reds? Or Hook?"

"Don't know," he says shortly. "I guess we'll find out soon enough. Do you know how to fight?"

"Fight? As in, I don't know," I gulp, "with swords and guns and stuff?"

"I'll take that as a no."

"I'll do my best if you give me weapons."

He stares at me. Then, with a soft curse, he flips one of his knives over and offers it to me, handle first. "Don't lose it," he warns. "These are my lucky knives."

"What luck have they brought you?" I mutter, gripping the knife, my eyes scanning the woods.

"Fuck all," he bites out, and I glance sideways at the dark scowl on his face.

"Then what—?"

Something huge bursts out of the cover of trees, coming at us.

"Watch out!" Peter roars, pushing me away and launching himself at the creature, leaping through the air like some superhero and stabbing his knife into it.

Reds.

Massive, gnarled forms, a cross-breed between grizzlies and robots, patches of fur and scales but also metal plates and gears, metal ridges jutting out of their backs. I see now why they call them Reds. The metal parts on their bodies are scarlet, as are their necks and chests.

As if splashed with blood.

Peter is a whirlwind of motion, stabbing and kicking, twisting and slicing, dark hair flying. I'm so stunned that I just stand there, watching, as he brings down, one, two, three Reds, even as more come lumbering out of the tree line.

I never expected him to be so... efficient.

So good a fighter.

I guess... with him acting so crazy and violent, I never thought he could pull himself together like that and become a... a killing machine.

Then again, crazy and violent *is* the definition of a berserk warrior, isn't it?

And I realize that I can't see his shadow swirling around him. He and his shadow right now are one.

Just like they were when he fucked me on the bed.

A growl alerts me to the fact that daydreaming while monsters rush you isn't exactly the best idea. The knife is shaking in my hand.

Or rather, it's my hand that's shaking. My arm. My torso. My entire body.

This is a different kind of fear. Not arousing at all. I realize it's because tied up in bed, I... I trust them not to hurt me. To give me what I need even as I protest, but not to acutely cause me pain, whereas this...

This is true danger.

The monster is coming at me and I'm frozen on the spot. Ice is running through my veins. My limbs feel frozen.

I lift my hand with the knife and it feels like I'm moving through water—*dark water closing over me, hands grabbing my ankles, pulling me down, no air in my lungs, instead a burning pain that makes me scream and choke and drown*—

"Run!" Peter yells but I can't move. Because for the first time, I see the Reds' face, and looking past it, more coming.

I can only stare at them, frozen—human faces, even if grotesquely twisted, familiar faces.

The same face, in fact, repeated over and over on every monster.

A female face.

Which looks too much like my own face for comfort.

"Goddammit," Peter is hollering, "move your pretty ass!" He turns and races toward me, grabbing me around the waist as he goes, lifting me up. "Have you gone deaf?"

Definitely not, because the sounds—the growling, crashing, the pounding of Peter's feet, the uneven thudding of his heart against my side are way too loud, even through the numbness and the pulse thundering in my ears—but they feel oddly distant.

Everything feels distant.

He's running pretty fast for a guy carrying a girl clutched to his side, I think, and of course that's when he stumbles and almost falls. He staggers a few more steps and stops, panting harshly, his hold on me loosening until my feet touch the ground.

"Fuck," he breathes and turns around, lifting his knife again. "See anything?"

"No." I scan the trees. We're standing in what looks like the grounds of a burned-down factory, just like the one near home back in the real world. The similarities don't surprise me anymore. Not much, anyway, after the small initial shock of recognition. "Did we lose them?"

"Perhaps." His frown tells me he's not convinced, but he doesn't move. After a while, he presses a hand to his side. His fingers come away streaked with red.

"You're hurt."

He grunts something I don't make out. Drops his hand with the knife to his side.

"How bad is it? Show me," I demand.

"Are you a nurse now?"

"No, I just want to see if you're dying or if I need to put up with you for longer."

That brings a smirk to his lips as if my reply pleased him. "Are you sure? Not going to faint at the sight of blood?"

"I'm a woman," I remind him. "I see lots of blood every month. Fainting all the time would be inconvenient."

He looks slightly puzzled at that, too confused for a guy so intimate with female anatomy, but maybe he's just dazed. There does seem to be quite a lot of blood on his white shirt. When he shrugs it off, it clings wetly to his muscular chest and stomach, and I help him peel it away.

Through the blood smeared on his skin, his tattoos wind like serpents, spirals and labyrinths, abstract geometrical patterns webbing his flesh, and something inside me shivers and wonders.

But the gash on his side commands my attention more. It's deep, seeping blood as I watch, one end deeper than the other. A claw gouge.

"Looks like it will need stitches," I say absently, trying not to gawk at all those inked, smooth muscles, the planes and ridges of a chest that looks like it was sculpted by some ancient master.

"You mean like... embroidery?"

A snort escapes me. "Have you never gotten stitches for a bad wound? Didn't you ever get cut up in your life and had to go to the ER?"

"I've rarely been so careless. I was distracted."

"By the changes in the island?"

"No." He's gazing down at me, his eyes very dark. "By you."

A beat of silence throbs between us.

"Sorry," I whisper. "What did I do?"

"You didn't do anything. You just..." He makes a frustrated sound.

"I just, what?" The thin, dark scar I'd noticed before running down his neck from his ear ends over his heart—but there is another one, fainter, running over his ribs. I trace it with my fingertip and he draws a hissing breath. "Who did this?"

"The Fae. Kill me or crown me, they said. I survived the crowning. But not without a cost."

"What cost?"

"The cost is my memory... my soul."

I swallow hard. "Why would they want you to be king? You're human, like me. Or used to be."

He chuckles darkly. "As you say."

"Peter..."

"We're not the same. I was born in between, on the crossroad of liminal place and time."

"Meaning what?" I'm frustrated by his vague, ambiguous answers that aren't answers at all. "Tell me."

"I'm not inside nor out, not at night nor in the day, not of Fae but also not of man, not really born but delivered, not quite dead but not alive, either."

Like I said.

Frustrating.

His eyes glitter, pinning me to the spot. It feels as if he's looking inside my head and at the same time hoping, willing me to understand.

But he's wrong.

"What? I... I don't know what all this means," I whisper, bewildered.

And the intensity fades from his gaze. "All you need to know," he says, "is that I was never quite like you, girl... whatever your name is."

"You forgot my name again?"

His brow furrows. "I forget stuff. I have lived too long. The others joined me more recently. Tink, and then the Twins, Colt and then Wes. But Hook and me, we've been here from the start. He was brought here first, and then I joined him."

"And when was that? Why?"

He shakes his head. "I can't fucking remember."

"Peter—"

"*Fuck*. Listen. Know how it feels when you start a story in the middle instead of the beginning, then you turn back you find that all those pages are missing, or printed funny so you can't fucking read?" He shoves a hand through his dark locks. "In my book, more and more pages go missing all the goddamn time and... Fuck this."

He's still holding his bunched-up, bloody shirt and he throws it to the ground in disgust, turning away from me, but not before I see his face. He looks so dispirited and worn out, so lost that I reach for him, to touch and comfort him.

He lets me. Turns toward me, hauls me into his arms.

God. I am so stupid. I was wrong. The true danger wasn't the Reds. No, it's the monsters in my bed. It's Peter and the Lost Boys.

The true danger is how they touch my heart.

20

TINK

"Where the hell are they?" I pace the length of the sitting room, stopping at every turn to look out the window running one wall. "Where did they go?"

"Settle down, Tinkers." Wes is cleaning out his gun, a thoughtful frown on his face. "You're wearing a hole into the carpet."

"There's no carpet."

"Oh no," he quips, "then it's already too late. You've worn it down to nothing."

"You're not funny, Wes." I stop at the window, bury my fingers in my hair and pull. "Something's wrong. I can sense it."

"Really sense it, or is it only a dramatic line from the latest book you read?"

"I haven't read anything since the last Wendy went mad," I mutter.

"Hm." Wes gets up and comes to stand beside me, folding his arms over his chest. "I thought Peter only wanted to show her the changes on the island. Get her ideas on how and why this is happening."

"Why would she have any clue?"

"Don't underestimate her," Wes says.

"Why, because inexplicably her nightmares keep bleeding into Neverland?"

"Because she doesn't hate us." Wes shrugs. "Yet."

"Give her time. She will."

"We don't even know if she has time," Wes says grimly.

"Fuck." I lower my hands. "Peter is convinced she's the one. She apparently isn't hurt by the island, and manages to both make it shrink and get the Reds to break the anniversary truce, but that makes no sense because he fucked her. Hell, you two also fucked her, which should have erased her magic."

"Which leaves you," Colt says from his perch on the sofa. He isn't cleaning his gun. He's just been staring down at it, but now he's looking at me. "You haven't fucked her yet."

"Don't go there," I warn.

"We could distract you," Colt says, the relentless asshole. "Get you to loosen up."

"Fuck off."

"But you never want that, do you, Tink?" Colt goes on.

"No idea what the hell you're talking about."

"All that violence but not sex. Never sex. And yet you're no angel."

A laugh escapes me. It fucking hurts my throat. "*Angel*."

"Exactly my thoughts. And yet." Colt gets up, moving toward us, and suddenly I feel cornered between them and the window. "And yet, Tink." He places a hand on my arm.

"Get off me," I snarl.

"Grab him, Wesson."

"No." As Wes' arms close around me, a darkness falls over me. I thrash against him, howling like a banshee that's definitely in my bloodline, elbowing him and kicking at Colt— at the shadows holding me, torturing me, burning me from the inside out. "No, damn you, let me the hell go!"

"Easy, now. It's just that with Wendy, you seem calmer," Wes says. "When you lay on top of her on the sofa... I thought you'd gotten over whatever trauma it is you have."

"Fuck you," I breathe.

"Okay." Wes releases me, and Colt steps aside. I shove at him anyway as I stumble past him and head for the door. "Wait. Tink."

"You motherfucking asshole," I mutter. "Fuck you and your ancestors."

"I don't care about my ancestors," Colt says, his tone light and bemused. "Just you."

I'm frowning as I throw the door open. "Got a nice way of showing that you care."

"Tink." Wes is coming after me, hands spread, palms up. "Listen, I've been here for years and decades, and you never want to open up about your past. Something fucking happened, I just know it, it's so fucking obvious, but you won't let us help. You—"

"Help?" I stop and turn back around, panting. "*Help?* You've been here for *decades*, Wes. *Decades*. I have been here for fucking centuries. And not even Peter knows much about my past. Why should you?"

"Because," Wes says and swallows, the knot in his throat bobbing. His eyes glimmer like old gold. "After all the centuries, it's about time you talked about it, don't you think?"

I'm breathing hard. No matter what I do, I can't seem to be able to catch my fucking breath. "Stay back."

My broken half-shadow writhes about me. My magic sputters and sparks.

He lifts his hands. "Don't turn me into a frog, okay? I'm just saying, we wanna help, Tink. Both of us."

"You can't."

Wes grimaces. "And who can? Can Wendy help you?"

"No, I..." I shake my head. "Why her?"

"Because," he says slowly, as if to a dim-witted child, while

Colt remains silent, "she's a woman, and those who hurt you were men, weren't they?"

No, I can't breathe, can't fucking draw a single breath. When did I let my walls fall and now everyone can see right fucking through me?

With a curse, doing my best to rein my magic in, I turn and run out into the woods, hearing faintly behind me Wes calling out my name.

———

I'M RUNNING, THREADING AMONG THE TREES, WEAVING THE pattern of my panic. What the hell has gotten into the Twins? I can't talk about my goddamn past. Can't think of it.

It's not like I can completely escape it. It comes to me in my dreams. They aren't as bad as Peter's, I don't think, judging from his screams, but they're bad enough.

I've built a wall between the past and my mind. I'm not forgetting, it's not that. No, I have shut the past out deliberately.

It's for the best.

It's for my sanity.

We all suffered in different ways growing up with absent or twisted shadows. I never asked the Twins to share the burden of their childhoods, or Peter about how he ended up here. I mean, I know the broad strokes but not the details.

That's where the devil is, or so the mortals say.

"Stop running," I tell myself out loud. "Fuck, stop running now."

Ever wonder why I have no Shadow?

How it was torn away?

"Shut up," I whisper to myself, "shut up!"

Can't outrun the past. And you're not a little kid anymore. Back there, that was the Twins, dammit, not your ghosts. You're an adult. You have magic. You're damn dangerous.

Even Peter stays away—but fucking Wes had to go and put his arms around me.

He didn't know.

How could he? I've never told anyone the details.

Back to the devil you know.

The devil of a past.

And it's not helping that someone is grunting like he's having sex.

Goddammit, mind, stop making this up. I don't need the soundtrack. Keeping the wall up between my thoughts and memories is fucking hard enough as it is.

I rub my face, hit my head with my open palms, hoping to stop the sounds.

But they persist.

Oh, what the fuck. I know that voice.

Rage blasts through me. Talk about the mother of all bad timings. With the ghosts battling it out in my head, trying to make their escape and torment me, this is the last fucking thing I need.

And on top of that...

"Peter Pan, you fucker." I wade through the weeds off the path and see them almost immediately.

He has her bent over a rock and is fucking her from behind, the way he likes to fuck. I know how they all like to fuck—but I don't. Don't like to fuck, not unless it's all under my control, unless I lose control, and the aftermath is never pretty, so...

My mind shifts the scene, showing me dirty walls and floors, showing me fanged, snarling mouths dripping blood, echoing my own screams back at me.

"You, asshole," I growl, advancing on him. My magic punches into his back, piercing him like a hook, lifting him off his feet into the air.

I see his eyes widen, his arms windmilling—

"Tink, no!" she shrieks.

—and I slam him into a tree trunk, hard enough that bones audibly crack.

Peter slides down to the roots, slack like a puppet with the strings cut, head bowed.

"You killed him," Wendy says, her voice hushed. She turns and sits on the rock, pulling on the hem of the white dress I picked out for her. Her face is pallid.

"He can't be killed," I dismiss her worry. "But he can feel pain, and fuck him."

"He can't be killed?" she whispers with a frown.

"Surprise," I say flatly.

"What's the matter?" Peter breathes after a long moment, a way too long moment, lifting his head and coughing. Blood spatters his lips. "Because you can't fuck, you decided we can't, either?"

"You, motherfucker." I march on him, ready to beat him into a pulp, my hands sparking. "I'll fuck you up, alright."

"Whoa." He lifts a hand. "Slow down, Tinker. What's going on?"

"You bastard, you slept with her again!"

"And why wouldn't I?" he mutters.

"Yeah, why shouldn't he?" Wendy whispers.

"You never do that. You sleep with a chick once, you discard her like a used rag. That's what you said. Your exact words. *Used rag.*"

Peter has the gall to shrug. "So?"

"In all the centuries, you never looked at a girl twice, never went back for more."

Wendy makes a small sound and takes a step back.

"What's your point, Tink?" Peter asks.

"My point?" I want to crucify him on the tree. "My point is that... forget it. *Fuck.*"

"Are you jealous?"

I feel the blood draining from my face. "My fault for giving a shit," I mutter.

"Are you really worried about me, Tink?"

"What if I am? What do *you* care? What if all this worries me?" I twirl a finger in the air. "You didn't take Wendy because you thought she is the one, did you? You watched her, saved her, got attached to her. And then when she grew up, you were hard for her."

"Tink—"

"Stop thinking with your dick, Peter." I jab a finger at him. "I don't understand what is going on here, but whatever it is, it's not going to save the Island. It's not going to save us."

"Who says I hope to be saved?" He climbs back on his feet. "Who says we can be saved?"

"What? But I thought—"

"We tried. For centuries. For fucking centuries!" His voice is rising. Wendy shrinks back as his shadow pulses. "And what do we have to show for it? Might as well live for the moment. Forget the pain for a blissful hour. The island is shrinking. Soon we will be mermaid fodder and as for her..."

"What about me?" she whispers, still pale.

"There are many paths into madness," Peter says, not unkindly, but she flinches.

"Maybe she's not the one changing the island," I say. "Maybe she's just the last drop, the last wrong Wendy we have brought over."

"That *I* brought over, you mean," he says, bleak. "I failed. And I don't know if I can go back. My shadow is tearing me apart, Tink. It's shredding my mind. I don't know how much longer I can hold on."

Fuck.

21

PETER

P ainfully I stretch, my spine cracking as vertebrae pop back into place. Holding onto the tree trunk, I get back on my feet. I rub the back of my head.

Damned Tink and his magic. His strength. Sometimes I forget how powerful he is.

I forget too much.

Like... what the fuck, Tink *cares*? About me? Why would anyone? I mean, I know they all stuck around for a reason, but I thought... I thought it was to resolve this spell.

I didn't know any of them got attached.

That's a mistake. We can't.

Why are they all here anyway? Why stick with me, on this forsaken island in Neverland when they could be... home. In the human world or other parts of Faerie that aren't getting swallowed by despair and the waves.

I know the answer to that, dammit. They're here because... they don't have another home, do they?

The world has left them destitute, like me, destitute of goods and heart. Of family. Of anyone who gives a damn.

Somehow, I wish I was back in the human world, hunting

for a girl named Wendy to save us all. There I remember things. There, my shadow belongs to me, with me, it has my shape and my thoughts. It's only here that it warps out of shape.

"Peter," the girl says.

"Wendy." That has to be her name. All of them, all the girls I stalked and brought over were called that.

"You remember," she smiles.

"Not really."

Her smile falters. Probably not the best reply you can give to a girl you were just fucking. Then again, she knew when she kissed me that I didn't recall who she was.

"Come." Tink grabs her arm and hauls her to his side. "Let's go. Time for you to get off this island."

"What?" She's glancing from him to me, eyes wide. "For real?"

"*Tink*," I snap, annoyed.

"What? You have to take her back, Peter."

"Back?" I mutter.

"Don't pretend not to understand, asshole. Back to the human world."

I fold my arms over my chest. "Why should I?"

"You want her to die here?"

"She can save us," I tell him.

"She's destroying everything!"

Wendy hisses at us. "I'm not."

"The hell you're not!" Tink snaps.

"You mean the island?" I ask.

He doesn't reply, his gaze bleak and I think he's talking about something else.

It doesn't matter.

"I can't take her back," I say.

"Why not? Why not take her back?"

"Why not? Are you serious?" I glare at him. "Apart from the fact that every such trip tears my fucking shadow a little bit more, apart from the fact I just brought her over, Tink, and the fact that there's still hope—"

"There's no fucking hope!" he yells.

That brings me up short. Wait... Is Tink jealous? I step closer to him, lift a hand to his face. "Tink—"

He slaps it away. "Don't. Fucking don't."

Doesn't he know that I care for him, too?

Probably not. It's not like I ever show what I feel. Caught in a maelstrom of pain and fury, pulled this way and that by a shadow who wants to maim and kill, I'm rarely in the frame of mind to sit and talk and be gentle with anyone.

Which begs the question why I think I should do it now, of all times, as the island crumbles and my memory withers.

Maybe because she's here. She makes me feel... settled. Rooted. Located in space and time, even as I know it's an illusion.

"Wendy—" I start.

"Let me go," she whispers. Her eyes are too large, too wide, too dark. Why is she so scared? Her cheeks have paled to milky white and she's trembling.

That's when I notice Tink's power flaring again. It twines around him like a storm cloud, swirling with flashes of lightning.

"Stand down, Tinker," I mutter. "Let's discuss this."

"Discuss what? You can't even recall what we're trying to do here, can you?"

"What do you mean? We're trying to save the island, to save ourselves, to—"

"You don't *remember*!" he roars and sparks fly off him, stinging my skin.

"Remember what?"

"What this is all about."

"The island—" I start.

"Fuck the island!"

I stare at him. "What the hell, Tink?"

"Who are we trying to save? From what? Every time we go over this, but your memory has gotten so fucking bad you forget from one day to the next."

I blink. "What...?"

"You put us into this situation, Peter," he says, his voice shaking with anger. "You trapped us here to help you."

"What the hell are you talking about?" Peter snarls.

"You said, if we save her, we save ourselves, but that's not what it's all about, is it?"

"Save me?" she whispers. "From what?"

"From the island!" Tink shouts. "From the nightmare! From herself! You trapped us with a honey trap of hope and redemption. Look at us!"

His eyes are glowing and his hair lifts in a wind I can't feel, the pink streaks darkening. Dark lines rise on his pale skin, writhing like snakes.

She twists, trying to free her arm from Tink's grip. Lifting her other hand, she slaps him across the face.

"Let me go," she seethes. "I'm not a plaything for all of you to grab and push and bend over. Let me go, you freak!"

And Tink loses control, just like I did earlier. It was a matter of time, I think dimly, and he's been on the edge for far too long.

He roars again, his magic bursting out of him in a rolling wave that knocks me over. I crash to the ground, groaning as my still-healing spine protests.

It rolls over her, too, and I make an abortive grab after her.

"Wendy!" I yell as she's blasted away, rolling on the ground like a ragdoll. "Tink, what have you done?"

He's not hearing me.

He's marching on her, hands turned to claws, hair turned to the branches of a tree, his face becoming a dark mask of fury— the face of the old gods, the hideousness the Fae hide under their pretty façade surfacing. He's pulsing with power, every pulse sending the trees shaking, their leaves flying.

That's the power of the son of a Faerie King.

And they want *me* to be the king.

Fuck.

Bitter laughter bubbles up my throat—but then, my breath catching, I see her writhe on the ground. My laughter dies, joyless as it was.

"Wendy!" Cursing, hissing in pain, my back a thing of pure fucking agony, I manage to get on all fours and crawl toward her. "Wendy, are you okay? You asshole, Tink, she's not like us, oh fuck…"

But then I stop as she slowly sits up and gets on her feet. I stop, stock-still, as she lifts her head. Light blazes from her face, her neck, her hands.

I stare.

Blink.

Tink is still going after her, blazing like a night sky, his Fae nature all twisted up in anger, leading him, possessing him.

"Tink! Stop! Fuck, man, stop!"

He doesn't seem to hear me. He's a flare of darkness and I scramble to my feet, grabbing at him.

His magic sends a shockwave through me, shaking every bone in my body, rattling the teeth inside my mouth.

He doesn't have a shadow. He *is* a shadow made of power.

"Don't, Tink," I whisper as he turns on me, fangs bared, eyes all black like a demon's. "Don't."

"Yeah, Tink, don't," a new voice says and Hook emerges from the woods.

Alone.

Seemingly unarmed.

And I'm too fucking stunned to move, still holding on to Tink's arm, buffeted by his magic that's trying to liquefy my bones and warp my muscles into new forms, to tear my shadow clean off.

"Come with me," Hook says, reaching a hand out to Wendy, smiling.

The fucker is *smiling*.

"I don't know if I should go with you," she whispers. The light around her is fading. Was it ever really there or did I imagine it? "Why should I?"

"I can take you home."

"Home?" Her eyes brighten.

"No," I say, though my voice comes out garbled. "Don't listen to him. He can't do that."

"Peter!" The Twins arrive running, panting. "Tink! What the hell, man, you..."

Silence spreads as we all contemplate Tink's shadowy, pulsing form, the waves of magic expanding around him.

"Holy fuck," Colt says, succinctly, expressing all of our feelings.

And Wendy takes Hook's hand. His smile widens.

"Good move," he says even as we all lurch toward them. Nobody ever speaks of Hook's shadow, and there's a reason for that.

It's not his own. It's a leech, attached to him, forcing on him the will of the Fae. A foreign body, much like mine is starting to be. Hook gave up his shadow to become who he is.

The envoy of the Fae King.

The Mermaid Queen's pawn.

"Wendy!" I yell but she doesn't look my way. She's gazing at Hook as if he's her savior. "Wendy, no! Don't trust him!"

She doesn't reply.

And as Hook's magic envelops them, I lunge at them, and grab her other hand.

Blackness swirls around us, erasing the world.

22

WENDY

ook—*Jas*—is gazing at me with a smile and a kind gaze. He's handsome like an angel with his white-blond hair and grey eyes. His hand is firm around mine.

I've snapped. My courage is shattered. Can't stay on this island of lunatics a minute longer, even if Tink... even if what I'm seeing can't be real, even if it's all in my mind and Tink hasn't transformed into some kind of monster.

If it's all in my mind, then I need out, I need to wake up.

I think I hear Peter shouting something but I can't make out the words.

"Come," Jas says. "Let's get you home." He tugs on my hand and we step away from the four men staring at us, reaching for us. "You must have missed your family."

"I have."

"You must be worried sick about them."

I nod, then wonder if it's true—and why am I having doubts now?—but before I can think of anything else to say, Peter grabs my hand and pulls.

"No," he says.

"Let her go," Jas says. "Peter, let her go."

"Can't," Peter hisses between his teeth. "You know I can't. *You* let her go."

"Release her, Peter," Jas says, his jaw tightening. "Now."

"You heard him." I try to shake Peter's hand off. "Release me. Come on!"

"If you go back…" Peter's face twists in a grimace that looks like pain. "Then all will be lost."

"What do you mean?"

"He has a mission," Jas says, his gaze hardening, "don't you, Peter? To find the right Wendy."

"But right for what?" I insist.

"To save the world," Peter says.

"And that's me? I'm supposed to do that?"

"I don't know," Jas says. "Are you?"

"No way."

"Told you so," Jas tells Peter. "All this is bullshit. So, what's the harm in taking you back home, right?"

"Don't," Peter says again. "Don't do it, Hook."

"Great king you are," Jas mutters, his eyes narrowing. "Letting the Fae use you, not seeing the bigger picture. Condemning all your men to death."

"You're the one who doesn't see the bigger picture," Peter growls. "Wendy, don't go."

God, this is so confusing. They kidnapped me, kidnapped who knows how many other girls before me, and now they're all dead and buried.

Why would I stay?

"Jas," I breathe, "can you really get me home?"

His gray gaze flickers, softens. "Yes. I said so. I don't lie."

"Sure you can lie. You're not a Fae," Peter snarls. "No matter how badly you wish it."

"You think that's what I wish?" Jas says. "All this time, you think I've been fighting you for myself?"

"What then?"

"I'm trying to save you! All of you. And I'll do it if it kills me." His pale eyes darken. "Release her right now, Peter."

Peter blinks. His hand tightens more around mine. All color drains from his handsome face. "No, Jas. Don't do it. No!"

But something slams into him, throwing him back, and my hand... My hand begins to shimmer, turning ghost-like. It slips from his.

"No..." Peter whispers as he starts to fade, too.

"It's for the best," Jas says.

"You'll kill us, Hook," Colt says, his voice echoing. "She was supposed to be the one to save us and you're taking her away. Don't you see what you're doing?"

"Don't listen to them, Wendy," Jas says. "They're the ones who are blind."

"But..."

Everything is growing fainter and fainter—the trees, their faces. Their voices.

"Neverland will be swallowed by the sea," Peter says, his voice cracking. "The Mermaid Queen will take me. Wendy, wait!"

"I can't," I whisper, even if I feel my heart is breaking. "I can't wait, and I don't trust you."

With a curse, he pulls the chain with his pendant over his head and fumbles to get it over mine. "Wear this."

"What? No. I can't..."

But he manages to pull it over my head, the small acorn thumping against my collarbone, and then it all goes black.

———

I FLOAT IN THE BLACKNESS FOR WHAT FEELS LIKE A LONG TIME— and yet I don't feel any panic. It's a warm and welcoming blackness, which makes no sense but there you go. Nice warm void.

It feels familiar.

It feels soft and comforting.

"Hey," a woman's voice says and my lashes lift in shock. "Feeling okay?"

"...Charlie?"

"What, you think I'd leave you home alone after the scare you had?" My friend is sitting on my bed, twirling a lock of her hair around a finger and smiling at me. "No way in hell, girly."

"It's you." I sit up so fast black edges my vision and my stomach roils. "Ugh..."

She frowns. "Why don't you lie back down and I bring you some hot soup I made, huh?"

"Soup?"

"I know, right? Hidden talents. I saw it on a TV show and decided to make it for you. It has chicken nuggets in it."

"Chicken... *nuggets*?"

"That's right." She smiles brightly. "Don't knock it till you've tried it."

"And I had... a scare?"

"Oh yeah. Don't you remember? You were attacked on the street by a crazy hooligan who tried to grab you. Wanted to rob you, I guess."

"I was?" I pat my bed, my quilts, needing to convince myself they're real, that I'm back in my room. The small white roses on the blue fabric are reassuringly familiar.

"You fainted. Kept saying that the man tried to kidnap you and that rescued you."

I look up. "Who?"

Charlie taps a finger against her lips, deep in thought. "You said... that it was the junkie from across the street. But..."

"But what?"

"You came home alone," she says. "And he's not around anymore. I haven't seen him all day."

The junkie.

That rings a bell.

But that's... that's all. A tiny bell in my mind. Hazy images hang in between my thoughts like sheets on which a projector is throwing fuzzy pictures—trees, a seashore, a house.

Faces.

Monsters.

"You had nightmares," Charlie says quietly. "You didn't want to go to the police, you said, you wanted to go to bed so I tucked you in. They seemed... bad."

"Yeah," I whisper.

"You kept calling out for me. Broke my heart."

"I did? It did?"

She giggles, then claps a hand over her mouth. "Sorry. It's not funny. You just... seem so shocked by everything I say."

I shrug. Pick at the corner of my quilt.

"Well, I'm buying you pepper spray and I'm sticking to your side until the police catch the pervert," Charlie declares, all signs of mirth fading. "And I called your work and they said to take the day off, no problem."

"And you..." I start, not even sure what I want to say.

I remember running—but not on the streets, not in a town but among trees, the sound of the sea crashing in my ears, a strong hand wrapped around my wrist, blue eyes flashing.

Then more faces—all of them handsome, some smiling, some scowling, lit up by jumping flames.

"You have to face your fears. Those who fear are lost."

Who said that?

Just dreams.

"I'm staying right here with you," Charlie says, breaking through my thoughts. "Now, I'm going to heat up the soup, okay?"

I nod, reaching for my pendant, an ingrained gesture of comfort—and my fingers close around an unfamiliar shape.

I look down at the golden pendant resting against my collarbone.

"Oh, nice pendant," Charlie says from the door. "I never noticed it before. Is that an acorn? Where did you get it?"

"I... don't remember."

A snarl, a flash of dark eyes. "Wear this."

"How can you not remember?" Charlie asks.

"The cost is my memory... my soul."

God. It wasn't real. It can't have been. I was attacked on the street, that's what happened. Charlie has just explained it all to me. I've been here this whole time.

I'm in shock. I never met the Lost Boys and Hook. I never went to Neverland. My nightmares are all mixed up with stories I read as a child.

That has to be it.

Nightmares and memories given faces as I try to make sense of what happened, using a jagged storyline to frame them and give them meaning.

That's all.

Somehow as I slept, I linked events and symbols together, stringing them like beads on a necklace. I should write down all I remember in my dream log, before I forget it all. Maybe later they'll make more sense to me than they do now.

But the question remains... where did I get the acorn pendant?

And why does it feel so important?

———

I END UP STAYING HOME FOR TWO MORE DAYS WITH A FEVER.

Charlie diagnoses me with shock and maybe also a cold, and I don't argue with her. Her soup isn't all so bad and besides, all I want is to stay wrapped up in my blankets and try not to think and not to dream.

It mostly works.

But eventually I have to drag myself out of my cocoon and get back to work before I get fired. My boss already sounded pretty annoyed on the phone when I told him I needed more time. I guess supportiveness and business sense don't entirely go hand-in-hand.

So here I am, trudging through the gray morning to work—gray as the morning I was attacked, which I barely recall.

I still shiver as I cross the street, glancing over my shoulder, expecting someone to grab me at any moment—*a fanged mouth, claws for hands, a beastly shadow flickering on the walls, hands holding me down—*

"Wendy?"

I scream like a little girl, then twist around and run. I keep screaming as I go, almost crashing into a pole, then slipping in a puddle of water and falling.

Falling.

Still falling.

Suspended in mid-air.

A hand has grabbed my wrist in a steel grip, stopping me from crashing face-down to the sidewalk. A low voice says, "Wendy."

I stare up at him, my mind blank. "Do I know you?"

"It's me, Peter!"

Handsome face.

Dazzling blue eyes.

A powerful body.

Ink covering every bare inch of his skin and a thin black scar running from his ear down his neck, dipping into the V of his sweater.

It nags at me. Where have I seen it before? Where have I seen *him* before?

"You're the junkie," I whisper as it eventually comes to me. "From across the street."

A bark of a laugh escapes him. "That's all you remember of me?"

"What else?" But his hold on my wrist is eerily familiar. I frown down at it as he rights me, sets me back on my feet.

"Wendy, you have to remember," he says, his voice a deep rumble I feel in my bones.

"Remember what?"

"Neverland. The island. *Us*."

"I imagined it all," I whisper. "I dreamed it all up. It was a dream."

"No, it wasn't." He lifts his other hand, uncurls his fingers and something glints on his palm.

My silver thimble.

"Where did you get that?"

"You dropped it in the woods. I found it after you left. Please, Wendy, you have to remember. You have to come back."

"Come back? Are you crazy?"

"Maybe. Damn, I can't stay for long. I'm using the last of my strength to be here. Wendy, if you don't come back to us, we're all going to die. Everything you know will be gone, all the people you love, gone."

I laugh. "Nonsense. I don't even know who you are."

"I'm Peter Pan. And my friends are Tink, and the Twins. And do you remember Hook? He sent you back here."

"Hook," I whisper, frowning as I try to recall. "No, I..."

"Use the acorn I gave you." Peter takes my hand, wraps it around the golden acorn hanging around my neck. "Think of us. Think of the island. *Remember*, Wendy."

"Oh, God." I gasp as sharp shards of memory slice through me.

I remember pleasure.

I remember fear.

I remember pity.

"This acorn is your link to me," he says. "To us. Don't you want to help us?"

"You tied me up," I whisper, choking on fear and anger, shame and desire. "And used me."

His eyes darken. "You liked it," he breathes.

I want to deny it but something in me won't allow me to lie. Still... "You're monstrous. Your shadows... and the mermaids, the Reds... Hook..."

"You remember." He grins, and it transforms his face from handsome to breathtaking, like he's some king of old come to life. "Wendy, you're remembering!"

"Doesn't mean I want to go back," I mumble. "Here is my home. I have my family, my friends."

"Fuck." His lashes lower. "I see."

My heart clenches in my chest as I look at his bowed head. I remember... more. I remember how I felt around him, around them. The glimpses of who they really are, of vulnerability and pain, drawing me in.

But is it enough?

"If you change your mind," he whispers, "take the acorn in your hand and call out my name three times."

"That's all?"

His face flickers, like a projection, like he isn't really there. His hand over mine seems to lose density, to turn into fog and smoke, and that's familiar, too. "Say you believe in us, Wendy, and we will appear to you."

"This isn't a fairytale!"

"No, you're right, it isn't." His smile is tight and bitter and sharp like a blade when he lifts his eyes once more. "I don't believe in fairytales. But I, for one, believe in you."

"All of this has happened before, and it will all happen again."
— J.M. Barrie , Peter Pan

ACKNOWLEDGMENTS

I suck at this. I owe so much to so many people. I want to thank my amazing betas – Kamisa Cole, Darcy Bennett, Fawn Fields, Lainey Da Silva, Saundra Wright. I want to thank everyone in my group and everyone on social media who have been so kind to me.

I suppose this is more of a dedication rather than just a thank you: to all of you kind readers and amazing people, all my words are for you. I hope you enjoy them.

LORD OF SHADOWS (BRUTAL NEVER BOYS 2)

I hope you enjoyed King of Nothing! The story continues in Book 2 (Lord of Shadows) and it's coming out on May 21 2023, so mark the date.

———

After escaping Neverland and its mad lords, who in their right mind would ever wish to go back?

My memories from the island torment me. I am worried about Peter, Jas, and the other Lost Boys, no matter how badly I want to deny it. Coming back to my own world hasn't given me the relief I'd expected.

I miss them.

I miss what we did together.

I miss being with these men who understand me, understand what I need and give it to me, no questions asked, no regrets, no shame.

Leaving them, I was aware I might be signing their death warrant, but I was selfish. I thought I was happy in the human world.

But the truth is, I don't think I am. The only place I've ever felt safe and content and right in my own skin was with them, on the island. In Neverland.

So when Peter Pan appears below my window, I jump at the chance to go back.

Call me crazy.

I must be.

Will things be like before? Will I be able to help them? Will I face my fears? What about my feelings for them?

And their feelings for me?

OTHER BOOKS FROM MONA BLACK!

Book 1 in the Cursed Fae Kings series (standalone fae romance novels series):

<u>The Merman King's Bride</u>
A cursed King of Faerie
A princess betrothed to a man she doesn't love
A kiss that will change everything

The last thing Princess Selina expects to find in the lake in the woods is a handsome merman. His name is Adar and he saves her, teases her, kisses her, and tells her she could break his curse.

Because, as it turns out, he's a Fae King, cursed to remain in merman form until he finds a princess to kiss him.

But one kiss is not enough and Selina has other problems.

Such getting engaged to a prince she isn't sure she even likes, let alone loves. Marrying him and having his children is not on her list of favorite things.

And now she's falling for the merman.

He's everything she could wish for in a man. Handsome, protective, kind. Except that he is Fae. And has a fishtail.

Still, she can't stop thinking about him. Keeps going back to him. Craves his kisses.

Would gladly have his babies.

Is this a spell, or is it love? Can she break the curse and save Adar? Will there be a happy ending to their story?

All a girl can do is try. After all, true love is worth fighting for and Selina knows she has found it.

This book is standalone novella-length NA romance fantasy novel, featuring mature situations with some dark themes and adult language. It is a retelling of the Frog Prince, with all the emotions, romance, spice and heat.

———

A completed Paranormal Reverse Harem series! Welcome to Pandemonium Academy!

"Of Boys and Beasts"

One's a werewolf with an ax to grind

Two's a vampire with a heart of coal

Three's a demon with a taste for pain

Four's a fae with a past of woe

Five's a girl who will take them down all

In revenge for the pain they've sown

So what if they're gorgeous? They must atone…

My name is Mia Solace. You know, the girl who will take them down all? That's me.

When my cousin is returned to us by Pandemonium Academy in a glass coffin, in an enchanted sleep she isn't expected to wake up from, I grab her diary and head to the academy myself.

Because her diary, you see, tells of four cruel boys who

bullied her and broke her heart until she sought oblivion through a spell.

Four magical boys, because that's the world we live in now, heirs of powerful families attending this elite academy where the privileged scions of the human and magical races are brought together in the noble pursuit of education.

As for me, I cheat to get on the student roster, and once I'm in, well… it's war, baby. I'll get those four sons of guns, steal their secrets, make them hurt. I'll transform into an avenging angel for my cousin, for all the girls they've wronged, and I bet there are plenty of those.

While growing up, my cousin was my only friend. Now I'll be her champion.

Only these boys aren't exactly as I pictured them. Devastatingly handsome, deliciously brooding, strangely haunted, they're getting under my skin and through my defenses.

Kissing them surely wasn't part of my plan…

Getting into bed with them even less.

ABOUT MONA BLACK

Mona is a changeling living in the human world. She writes fantasy romance and reverse harem romance, and is an avid reader of fantasy and paranormal books. One day she will get her ducks in a row and get a cat so she can become a real author.

Check out her paranormal reverse harem series Pandemonium Academy Royals, and her fantasy romance series Cursed Fae Kings.

Books by Mona

Fairytale Retellings
The Merman King's Bride (Cursed Fae Kings 1)
The Beast King's Bride (Cursed Fae Kings 2)
The Feral King's Bride (Cursed Fae Kings 3)

Paranormal Reverse Harem
FREE Prequel to of Boys and Beasts - Of Girls and Stories
Of Boys and Beasts (Pandemonium Academy Royals 1)

Of Beasts and Demons (Pandemonium Academy Royals 2)
Of Demons and Witches (Pandemonium Academy Royals 3)
Of Witches and Queens (Pandemonium Academy Royals 4)